GRACE NICHOLS was born in 1950 in Georgetown, Guyana, where she grew up. She took a Diploma in Communications from the University of Guyana and worked as a reporter and freelance journalist. She came to Britain in 1977 and since then has published a number of children's books and two collections of poetry. Her first, *i is a long memoried woman*, was the winner of the 1983 Commonwealth Poetry Prize, and her second, *The Fat Black Woman's Poems* was published by Virago in 1984. Grace Nichols lives in Lewes, Sussex, with poet John Agard and her daughter Lesley.

In *Whole of A Morning Sky*, her first adult novel, Grace Nichols richly and imaginatively evokes a world that was a part of her own Guyanese childhood.

were some who ran one way.
were some who ran another way.
were some who did not run at all.
were some who will not run again.
And I was with them all,
when the sun and streets exploded,
and a city of clerks
turned a city of men!
was a day that had to come,
ever since the whole of a morning sky,
glowed red like glory,
over the tops of houses.

Martin Carter

no matter wha race
no matter wha creed
is all ahwe taste
de sweat o we brow
is all ahwe bleed
fo de bitter cane
is all ahwe feel
a similar pain
is all ahwe share
a similar need
is all ahwe hoping
is all ahwe groping
is all ahwe dreaming
an is all ahwe
gon wake up an burn
if we don't learn . . .
if we don't learn . . .

John Agard

Whole of A Morning Sky

Grace Nichols

To the memory of
my mother and father

Published by VIRAGO PRESS Limited 1986
41 William IV Street, London WC2N 4DB

British Library Cataloguing in Publication Data
Nichols, Grace
Whole of a morning sky.
I. Title
813 [F]   PR9320:9.N/
ISBN 0-86068-774-0
ISBN 0-86068-779-1 Pbk

Printed in Great Britain by Anchor Brendon
of Tiptree, Essex
Typeset by Goodfellow & Egan at Cambridge

You run fast alongside the red brick public road, feet flashing over grass and earth and stones. Today they're encased in white nylon socks and brown polished shoes because today you're leaving the village. For good. Still your legs move easy. You were born on this piece of earth. On these open spaces.

A minute ago you darted out of the shingle-roof cottage, possessed by the urge to see the old backdam one more time. The weeks of restless excitement now swim before your eyes like a block of pure loss.

You run, past the small cakeshop, covered in a skin of red dust, shelves almost empty, only a few jaw-breaking pieces of cornsticks, some coconut buns, perhaps some mauby.

You run, past the wide stretch of water on your right, always tempting you to run straight in and become part of it. Past a few more houses, set far in from the road, half-hidden by the branches of tamarind and mango trees. Past Cousin Nel, the biggest house in the village, unpainted, dark, a heap of coconut husk and shells at the front. The smell of copra and coconut oil from the rambling uneven yard.

You come to the narrow dam swinging off from the road, the familiar turning, feet now crushing lumps of dark moist earth, leaving deep footprints behind.

You come to the ditch covered with floating, slimy moss. You take it with a flying leap, as usual scorning the heavy wooden plank across it. The earth this side covered with bramble and other bush. The bramble engrave your arms with thin scratches, strings of sweetheart attach themselves to your socks. A green iguana dart across your path like a big lizard and disappear with a rustle into the green.

Then you come to the long wooden fence and squeeze yourself through the narrow gap. A few more yards and you're standing in your portion of the backdam. No, not your portion any longer. Your father sold it less than two weeks ago to that old terror, Mr Watson, always running somebody off his land, putting red paint on the mangoes on his tree to scare off people. Everybody in the village own a piece of backdam.

You stand there breathing in the damp musty smell of the earth and trees, half-stifling half-sweet. The earth is covered in old leaves. You gaze at the trees around you. The fat twisting mango tree already bearing some tiny green mangoes. The thought come that they'll hardly be ripe before August.

But the jamoon tree laden with bunches of small purple fruits, deep purple, almost black looking in the morning sunshine. Today you don't feel like eating any, but against your will your hands reach out to circle the smooth white trunk. You shake hard, starting a downpour of jamoons and pieces of dry mud from the marabunta nests you've just shattered. The jamoons fall, splashing the earth with their bloody juice and the brown marabuntas overtake you, as if your body is a kind of magnet.

You never shake the jamoon tree. You always use

2

the long wooden stick with the nail at the end to coax down the bunches of fruit. Today you'd forgotten.

You leave, running blindly from the stings of the spiteful marabuntas, some still clinging to the skin of your neck and face.

As you head home you feel the hot burning, the slow spreading swelling. Then you hear your father calling, 'Gem, Gem.'

The family bags and suitcases already out at the gate. Everything set for Georgetown. You see them all through a haze of tears.

1

It seemed as if they'd spent much more than ten years in the village. The village, which was just thirty miles outside of Georgetown, was low and flat and this could have been the reason for the ironic name, 'Highdam'. Lowdam, Mud-dam or Crabdam would all have been better.

Highdam gave the impression of being more water than land. But this wasn't really so. It only looked that way because the water, brown, heavy and smooth, was right up front while the dry pasture lands and stretches of fruit trees lay at the back of the village and weren't readily seen.

Gem's father, Archie Walcott, had gone to Highdam to take charge of what surely must have been the rowdiest school in the British colonial educational system. But it was there and the conscience of the administration was clear. They had provided for the people.

The people of Highdam saw in the school, a low, narrow discoloured building, not so much a place of learning as a symbol of their own importance. The nearby villages had no schools, so the people who lived there, mostly East Indians, were forced to send their children to the Highdam Methodist School. In a way they valued it more.

Highdam itself was looked on as a black community, but

many of the people were a blend of more than one race, skins ranging from light and reddish browns to shiny charcoal. Everybody was somehow blood-related to everybody else and it wasn't uncommon to find nieces expecting for uncles, and quite common for cousin to marry cousin, making them a bit clannish and unruly, Archie Walcott thought.

East Indian cartmen had their mango carts toppled over just for fun when passing through Highdam. Drivers going through the village had to be extra careful about knocking over cows and sheep. No questions were asked. The driver was simply dragged from his vehicle and beaten up. So they took it easy on the Highdam home stretch.

In a way Highdam expired the breath of raw life. The air was always saturated with the vapour of the salt water, and always there were many scents. Of fresh mud and fish, cows and pigs and scalding milk. When the rain fell, the heavy soil sizzled and the vegetation steamed, making everything into a living sea of odour.

Farming and fishing were the mainstay of the village, the women mostly catching the fish and shrimps and the men looking after the soil and cattle. The women tied their heads and hauled for shrimps in groups, standing waist deep in the water, laughing and exchanging talk as the water moved between their legs like heavy brown silk, caressing their thighs and hips with a voluptuous pleasure.

When the salt water came right in, fish like huri and patwa floundered at their very back doors. Children were in their element when this happened. With little or no effort they grabbed the slippery, half-stunned fishes with bare hands, gleefully popping them into old baskets and tins.

Catching crabs was fun too. When the water receded, leaving a patchwork of cracks and holes, people stole along the shoreline just before dawn. While the stars looked down from their faraway isolation, they padded the shore with torchlights, buckets and grassknives in hand. Everybody spoke in hushed voices, watching the flat red crabs

5

emerge hesitantly, then deftly they brought their grass-knives down with a fatal crack.

After a day in the backdam or pasture, the men, returning from their solitary ways, trudged home late in the evening with the cattle or hoe, scorched and mud-dried but not without a sense of accomplishment.

Apart from a few late-nighters who visited friends to old talk (usually about jumbies and other kinds of supernaturals), most people retired to bed by eight, leaving a dark village with the occasional far-off sound of a braying donkey.

Life was like that when Archie Walcott went to Highdam with his family. At the time he was still in his prime and had gone about rehabilitating the school with his new firm hand.

Tall and straight with dark brown distinctive features, it was his eyes that had caught his wife. They were greyish brown and filled with an indescribable quality that had something to do with pain.

Archie was given a shingle-roofed cottage that faced the water to live in and his only regret was that it was in the school compound which made it seem like an extension of the school.

In those early days he faced many conflicts. He found both teachers and pupils 'a lawless bunch', as he liked to describe them. The pupils, though he could hardly consider some of them by that mild term, had the gall to present themselves for classes after staying away for months on end. They gave no excuses but took their places behind the shaky desks, legs spread defiantly apart, patches of bare brown and black buttocks pressed down into their seats.

The women teachers who lived nearby, as they nearly all did, divided their attention equally between teaching and cooking pot at home. They saw nothing wrong in putting some sums on the board and slipping home, then slipping back in again.

At registration time teachers called pupils by their nicknames. 'Mother-Mice?' a teacher would call and a plump little girl, fitting the description to a 'T', with her protruding tummy would immediately stand up, answering, 'Present, Miss'. It was also common to hear names like Man-Man, Boy-Blue, Robin-Redbreast or whatever emerged out of the village imagination. Archie himself was christened with the name 'Turkey Cock' though it was a long time before he became aware of it.

When it rained hard the entire schoolyard became a brown sea with the dingy white school and cottage suspended in the middle. At these times teachers left their shoes at home and paraded barefoot before their classes. Some of the East Indian children came rowing to school in small overcrowded boats. There was a lot of noise and laughter when they fell overboard and were fished out dripping.

In the mid-days sheep, goats and pigs stormed the schoolyard. It was the custom of the children who ate in school to give them their 'left-left' food.

Archie Walcott called many staff meetings. He spoke long and earnestly. He let it be known he would stand no nonsense. He was amazed at the teachers' habit of slipping in and out of school. He believed in a full day's work for a full day's pay. Teacher Mary, the stout, high-bosomed lady who acted as head prior to his arrival, listened to all his new plans and instructions in an ominous silence, arms folded, nostrils flared to indicate her resentment.

He said that teachers had to walk with their shoes on at all times and must refrain from calling children by their nicknames. They had to start preparing 'Notes of Lessons' again and submit them for inspection. He insisted on punctuality. Thrice a week he conducted the school in singing, waving his cane like a wand.

Pupils who stayed away for long periods without a good excuse would be written off the register, he told the entire school. He wasn't concerned if they had to help their parents in the rice field. Education was more important than rice and coconuts. Once education was in their heads nobody could take it away from them.

More than half of the desks and benches were broken or shaky. He managed to get some new desks and benches through the Methodist manager. He didn't know how they expected these things to last forever.

Classes which formerly ran into each other in a haphazard fashion were separated by blackboard screens. Within a term of taking over, one of the older bullies was expelled. Archie ignored the sinister repercussions.

One morning he woke to find a dead dog lying stiff across the front door of his home. Two weeks later he noticed that his front door seemed to be perforated by a lot of small holes. On closer inspection, digging a small screwdriver into one of them, he discovered that they were made by shotgun pellets. And one morning when he went across to school he found that the platform where he sat was covered in fresh cow dung.

After this initiation, however, things began to calm down and with the help of his Sunday sermons and his wife's charm the family fitted into the fabric of the village.

Clara Walcott had plenty of charm – some people had it and some people didn't. The women took to her because she looked at them with original eyes. She also laughed a lot. In fact, she had the greatest difficulty in controlling her laughter which always came on those solemn occasions when she knew it was the last thing she ought to be doing, a childhood throwback which she hadn't outgrown. Sometimes she saw it as a kind of disease she had to battle with. Burning with embarrassment, she would bite her lower lip until a deep spot of blood showed through the sensitive skin.

She had to slip through the side door of the school the very first Sunday they attended church there. The preacher, a short stocky red man, kept on imploring them not to be caterpillars but to be butterflies. 'Let us nat be content with the life of sin and darkness, my friends. Let us strive towards de higha life. Let us not be content to be kyatta-pillas. Don't be a kyattapilla, my friends. I say be a butta-fly,' he screamed.

Archie had resigned himself to her laughter, treating it the way one would treat the sudden giggling fit of a small child, simply waiting until it had spent itself.

It was the water that gave shape to the land, the water that softened the hot dry landscape. In the mornings Clara stood at the back window and watched the cows swimming across the water to graze on the higher side of the pasture. Small boys held on to cowtails and were carried along with them. White gauldings, skimming the water for small fish, sometimes followed the swimming cows, swooping down on them to pick the ticks from their backs.

It was always the people who made Clara like a place or not and she liked the Highdam people. She liked the women. They spoilt her, bringing her a share of fish and shrimps whenever they went hauling. They liked her craving for womantalk and roots magic, the way she sat there drinking in each word, her eyes imbuing them with a feeling of specialness long forgotten.

Rose, who lived across the road, came over almost every day, her bumptious behind shifting behind her, her husky-voiced 'Eeeee Oooooh' singing her arrival.

Rose told her of the times between she and her dead husband, Balty. He was a pork-knocker when she met him. She was young and brazen at the time. When people hear she was going to marry him, they say she now meet whey she going. She never meet another man with a tool like him. After they marry he lock her in the house for three days. For three days she din't see the road. All he could think of was wife and more wife. Some of the young boys in the village used to pass the house up and down, pelting stones on the roof and bawling out, 'Youall come outa dere.' She feel so shame to walk the road after. But that

9

wasn't all. The man used to thief things and give her. Gold chain, gold bracelet, gold earrings. When she walking down the road with them proud-proud, people would come up to her just like that and unhook dey earrings and chain. They wasn't really vexed with her, they only wanted their jewellery back. Then when the man come home and see her standing there goldless he would sigh and seh, 'Rosie, they tek am? I did thief am. I did thief am.'

Archie didn't like Clara becoming so familiar with the Highdam people. Already the women had started to call her by her first name instead of Mrs Walcott.

Once he walked into the bedroom and found Rose anointing Clara's belly. Rose looked uneasy but went on massaging the soft, supple, creamy flesh which she was treating for narah, her short expert fingers moving with slow circular motions around the uneven dome, an open bottle of coconut oil beside the bed, and a piece of string which she had used for measuring between Clara's navel and nipples.

Archie glanced at his wife's face and was surprised to see that it was free from embarrassment. He pursed his lips and left the room, feeling on the edge of all this womanness.

They would do anything for her, men and women alike. She always had this effect on people. Archie resented all the time she spent with these women, always in his house, and was annoyed with the fact she thought them so important. He had caught her picking lice from Vee's head, sitting there on the back steps with her dress folded between her legs just like them, parting the hair and carefully picking out each louse and putting it into a small cocoa tin.

But she wasn't like them, he thought, and it had nothing to do with the lightness of her complexion or her neat features and compact small body. There was a kind of refinement that seemed to absolve her from anything, even picking lice. It was a quality of humaneness, a generosity of herself, that was strange to his own nature.

Maybe that was why they liked her. He didn't know. At times he was cynical. She was a good-looking woman, fifteen years younger than he was and her own carefree nature made the difference seem even greater. Also, she didn't feel herself better than anyone, so who wouldn't like her?

Whenever they quarrelled he told her that life had been too easy for her. The only child of doting parents, she didn't have anything to do but play the piano and entertain her friends in their city home, he would say.

They didn't quarrel often but whenever they did he was left shaken by her fury. All her resentments, which nobody would think she could harbour, came to the surface. A blue vein rose up in her forehead. Her hands shook, picking up and putting down things. Her wide mouth with its touch of sensuality curled with scorn, her voice mocking. She knew only too well why life had given her such a good childhood. It was making up in advance for the hardships she knew she was going to face with him.

On moonlight nights your room pale, like just before morning. At times you're tricked by it, thinking it almost morning, but then you always remember.

You remember him out there too. Standing with his legs astride the road. Tall-tall, with his throw-back head gazing up at the moon. Head almost touching the moon. But only a fool would try to pass between his legs. Only a fool who want to die would try to slip past between them and give him the chance of snapping his legs together, crushing them flatter than a bake. That was the moongazer for you.

And outside you know the water is a smooth silvery plain. You could see her, the fair maid, combing the strands of her long hair with her comb of pure gold. If she drop the comb, as they're always doing, and if you happen to find it next morning then you have the chance of becoming the richest person on earth, because she'll give you anything to get it back. Anything.

Jumbies, on the other hand, like dark night so you have to be careful about that too. Like if you're coming home late one night and a jumbie following you (you know this from the swelling in your head), you mustn't go through your door backing him. Turn around and walk in back to front, facing him, giving a long suck teeth. Jumbies don't like kindness. You have to curse them and tell them 'bout their rotten navel. You know because your mother treated a jumbie kindly once and nearly died for it.

That was years ago when she was getting you. She told you the story many times. You were nearly not born.

It was an afternoon around sixish when darkness was just beginning to come. Your mother was between two minds. Whether to use the toilet bucket in her bedroom or to go all the way down to the pit latrine which was right at the back of the yard, behind the school.

As it was still fairly light she decided to use the latrine and walked slowly down with her round heavy belly. But even before she got there she could see that the door of the latrine was half open. But she didn't take it for anything and when she got there she was just about to push the door right back and step inside when she saw this old East Indian man, all dressed in his white dhoti, sitting on the seat.

She was embarrassed and pulled back the door very quickly, saying, 'Goodnight, Oh, I'm very sorry.' Then she turned and began to make her way quickly to the house, because the strangest feeling was coming over her, as if she was being stifled by tobacco fumes. And suddenly she remembered that the man sitting on the latrine had no feet. After that she knew nothing more. It was Dinah who found her, lying near the foot of the steps in a dead faint.

When the Highdam people heard about it next day they quarrel with her for being so stupid. A woman expecting had to be extra careful. Evil spirits were always on the lookout for a new body to enter. She should have cursed the old wretch stinking.

13

And Aunt May make you feel frighten about losing your shadow. People have three shadows, she say. A long one, a medium-size one and a short one. Evil people could trap one of your shadows, making you get sick, keeping it until you got finer and finer, like a stick, until you died.

2

As a child Archie was very devoted to his mother. He was her one child, born and raised on the country's windswept Essequibo Coast. His mother was a tall, dark woman, full of the qualities of the women at that time, faith and forbearance, cut and contrivance. She had a little East Indian blood in her, maybe a little Amerindian too, according to her friends. She wore her long, thick black hair in a fat roll at the back of her head.

Archie's father was a carpenter, an African man who already had a child by a wealthier coloured woman when he married Archie's mother. The wealthier woman's family, it appeared, didn't want him to have anything to do with their daughter.

Like most of the earth's people, they were very poor and after school Archie would work in a blacksmith's shop to bring in a little extra. He received twelve pence a week. But in spite of the poverty, his mother insisted that he should wear shoes to school, unlike the other schoolboys his age. Archie did his best to care for them for her sake. He restrained himself from kicking the bricks along the bricky public road and walked on the smoother parts. This and the shoes made the other boys feel he was a mother's boy, a sissy.

They taunted, provoked and pushed him. This went on for quite a while. Archie knew that complaining to his teacher or mother was useless. So one day he decided to pretend that he was going mad which the boys didn't give him credit for. He pulled out his leather belt from around his waist and began to chase them all across the country-side, lashing them wildly about their heads and backs, lashing and lashing, until all the weeks and months of repressed anger had come out, leaving him completely exhausted.

After that they left him alone. One or two even became his friends.

Then his father built a cakeshop under the house and things were a little better, but shortly after his mother died. He was twelve at the time, big enough to feel the weight of his loss.

And when he was in a particular frame of mind Archie would relate what happened to him shortly after his mother died:

One dark rainy night he was doing his homework at the table with the aid of a wicker lamp. He was alone upstairs as his father was still below, building a new counter for the shop. The wind was making all kinds of strange noises, tearing at the flapping zinc sheet on their roof.

He was doing his best to concentrate on his arithmetic when he heard footsteps coming up the stairs. At first he thought they were his father's, but the steps sounded lighter. When nobody opened the door, however, he dismissed it as part of his childish imagination. But a few moments later he became uneasily aware of another presence in the room. He stopped working and sat very still but he could feel the presence behind him coming nearer and nearer.

Then he felt as if his head was getting bigger and bigger. His pen slipped from his clammy fingers and he picked up the familiar body odour of his mother, the odour she had after bathing and rubbing her body with coconut oil.

Without seeming to turn his head he saw her face behind him, her long black hair disarrayed. After that he knew nothing else.

The next morning he woke to find himself in a strange room. He was at his neighbour's house. When his father came to see him he told Archie what happened the night before. A beam in the roof of the house had caved in, falling across the chair where Archie had been sitting. His father had come running upstairs when he heard the crash and found him lying in a dead faint on the floor, only inches away from the fallen beam which might have killed him if he had remained in his chair. Somebody had been protecting him.

The story was always a marvel to the children because, as far as they knew, their father never lied. And his mother must have been sorry for having to frighten him for after that he only saw her in dreams and always she was distant and smiling.

But his father died too, only four years after his mother's death and he had no choice but to go to live with his half-brother, Jack, who was older than he and who came to see him from time to time. Jack's mother had never married and still lived with her own parents. They were all ambitious people who were determined to see Jack through a medical career. But they treated Archie kindly and his brother helped him with many things – English grammar, decimals and books – that were to see him to a teaching profession.

When his brother left for the USA to study, Archie was left on the threshold of life, a very lonely and sober young man.

He began teaching at a village school on the Essequibo coast and taught there for nearly ten years. Then he asked for a transfer to a city school, got one, and a few years later met his wife. He was thirty-two at the time. She was eighteen.

That his wife's upbringing was completely different to his

was clear to him from the beginning. She was nurtured on love and gaiety.

From the very first time Archie set eyes on her at the home of an old music teacher friend he could tell that. Love and gaiety were there in the soft tendrils that escaped from her two plaits and curled behind her creamy brown neck, in the sleeveless white dress that fell to her knees, in her round arms and laughter-suppressed mouth, in all her slim girlish freshness.

And when he began to visit her home, as he had in mind courting, he understood why she had blossomed the way she had: her father, a jovial, brown-skin major in the Police Force, was openly affectionate with her and her mother, an extremely charming and soft-spoken woman, seemed nothing but love.

They lived in one of the more elegant-looking houses in the Eve Leary compound where the higher officers in the Police Force were housed. The home, which was breezy and spacious, overlooked the Atlantic and the stretch of sea wall that was built to keep it out. It was a happy home, always full of visiting friends and relatives, laughing chattering people who were entertained with fruit cake and home-made ice cream.

But his visits hadn't always been easy for him. At times he felt uncomfortable and stiff. Clara and her girlfriends had a way of bursting into sudden fits of stifled laughter that he couldn't see the reason for most times, and one Sunday afternoon a cousin of hers, a blind young man of about her own age, played a trick on him.

Sonny, as he was called, seemed to have made up for his blindness by acquiring a special sense of direction and touch which he used to play practical jokes on nearly everyone he met. Unknown to the as yet uninitiated Archie, Sonny came across to where he was standing on the veranda and slipped an egg into the pocket of his baggy trousers. Later, when they went back into the drawing room he said to Mrs Harris, Clara's mother, that she had

18

better have a look at her eggs on the shelf as he had the feeling that somebody had stolen one.

Mrs Harris, who was accustomed to his pranks, got up to look and then laughingly admitted that one of her eggs was indeed missing.

Archie, who was puzzled by all this talk of a stolen egg and the laughter that had begun in anticipation of something, was even more astonished when Sonny slid over to where he was sitting on the sofa, pushed a hand in his pocket and came up with the only slightly cracked egg. 'I keep telling you, you must stop this habit of stealing other people's eggs,' Sonny said in an admonishing tone, his round face the picture of innocence and earnestness. They were all laughing so heartily, Clara almost slipping from her chair, that Archie had no choice but to join in.

Yet in spite of the laughter it seemed that she was drawn to the suffering quality in his face and not to the smooth boyish faces of the other easy-going young men she knew.

They were married, a big formal event which only a few of his relatives attended, and shortly after he was offered the post of headmaster at a school back in Essequibo. They went there with three weeks of the long August holidays still to go.

In those early days of marriage they went for long walks along the pitch-black coast road at nights, with their only light the huge stars that clung close to the earth, and the only sounds those of the mysterious Goat Sucker birds with their uncannily human cries of 'Ah-who-you Ah-who-you', and the pounding of the Atlantic on the shore.

Sometimes he would suddenly release her hand and run ahead a little, laughing in the darkness and trying to scare her. When a few moments later he jumped out at her she would pretend to be a bit annoyed, just to please him.

In the hot, slow, breezy days they lazed around the house eating their fill of oranges, mangoes and pineapples. He was surprised at himself for following her movements around the house, almost fearing that she would disappear.

19

It seemed as if they did nothing but sleep, eat and make love. His long limbs felt too reluctant and heavy to do anything else. He felt a bit ashamed of the glow on his own face. That she should see it. His body reached for hers with a silent intensity.

And she, having come with no preconceived notions, undressed for him unashamedly, and accepted his thrusting hardness like the savouring of some strange exotic fruit, its full flavour eluding her. It was only after the birth of her first child, Dinah, that she began to fully savour the taste. It was as if her little daughter had touched some tiny hidden secret spring as she made her way down, saying, 'Here mother, a little gift to compensate for all the pain. A gift, a gift, the unfolding of your own fount of pleasure.'

And Archie, so obsessed was he by his passion that one morning, a couple of years after their marriage, he sat at the breakfast table staring at her. Staring more than usual, at her face, her neck, her bosom. Then he said in a sudden voice, 'What would you do if I was to hit you, eh?' For he badly wanted to hit her. To slap her cheeks hard. To slap her for her own lovely childhood and his hard empty one. To slap her for the pain and jealousy she was already arousing in him.

They sat there staring at each other for a while, man and woman sizing each other up, testing each other. Different emotions chased across her face, but when her voice came it was very calm, 'Make sure that whenever you hit me you do a very good job of it,' she said. 'Make sure that you don't leave an ounce of strength in my body. Make sure that I can't get up again, you hear.'

Archie knew she meant it.

Your father. You remember him in his faded blue pyjamas, giving you a ride on his back once, but it all seem so long ago. In school you call him 'Sir' like all the other children, and every Sunday you and Anthony take turns standing before him, watching him trim the nails on each hand you hold out, cutting clean and careful with sharp little scissors. At night you like watching him light the gas lamp, the blue flame from the methylated spirits gently burning, he pumping and pumping until the little net sac was full of light. And when he come back from his evening walks with his feet stretched out before him, you're always the first to loose out his lacings and take off his shoes. But he'd hardly ever touch you. Not like your mother tickling you till you had to beg her to stop, running her hands up and down your back and under your foot. Playing she was a spider.

21

3

Apart from his headaches and bouts of melancholia which he had come to accept, Archie Walcott enjoyed the best of health at Highdam and health headed his list of priorities. He exercised every morning at the back window, breathing in deeply and he himself took the milk from the milkman – a thin East Indian brown-skin man. Archie held the pot while the milkman ladled out the slightly frothy looking milk, and his eyes tried to detect any suspicious tinge in its tone and texture. It was believed that some of the milkmen mixed their milk with trench water and somebody was said to have found a little fish which had slipped into theirs. To Archie fresh cows' milk was the panacea to all mankind's illnesses and he was concerned whenever he heard that the milkmen were fiddling around with it.

He also enjoyed going for long walks along the wind-swept public road, especially in the afternoon cool, just after the sun had disappeared in a fiery glow behind the courida trees. Sometimes passing through an East Indian village, he would glimpse a woman squatting over her mud fire and the faint scent of curry would mingle with the intoxicating coast breeze he loved so much.

He was never allowed to pass through one of these

villages with his hands empty. Some parent or pupil would always invite him in.

'You must tek something with you, Teach,' they would say as he was about to leave, plying him with fresh greens and vegetables, and sometimes eggs. He knew it was their way of making payment for the extra free lessons he gave their children in the afternoons. He admired the Indians but he didn't trust them. He didn't trust anyone completely.

And he couldn't deny that his sense of well-being was over-shadowed by what was happening in the country. Everywhere he could feel it. The political shadows blowing on the wind of change, drifting not only across Guiana but the whole Caribbean.

Mohabir, the newly-elected East Indian Premier who had won the first general elections to be held in Guiana, was showing himself to be more and more of a Marxist with each passing day. Whenever Archie's thoughts turned to politics, he felt a vague but heavy dread in the pit of his stomach which had something to do with the careful savings in his bank account over the years. He was plagued by the fear that his savings could be washed away by some zealous communist flood, bent on carrying it all away for distribution among the poor. And the thing was, he was the poor, coming from poor and only getting to where he was through his own determination and resourcefulness.

The Walcotts had three children: Dinah the eldest, bright, self-confident, moody, passing all the exams there were to be passed, and starting to teach at the Highdam School when she was only fourteen. Gem and Anthony, the younger ones who disappeared for hours on end, poking at the crappos at the bottom of their pit latrine with long sticks; digging up earthworms; looking for bird's eggs; swimming in a shallow muddy pool and contracting ring-worm.

'Moneybush good for getting rid of ringworms and eczemas on the skin,' preached the Highdam women. 'Soak it down in a tub of hot water, let it cool down, then bathe the children, crushing and rubbing the small leaves all over the children skin. Toya boiled down with Daisy good for cold. Sweetbroom for washing out the inside and keeping it clean. Lemon-grass for keeping the body cool.' Clara's favourite was lemon-grass, infusing the whole house with that lovely lovely steamy scent whenever she boiled some.

The children didn't take after him, Archie thought. Like their mother, they had no order about them. Nothing could ever be found in the house when it was wanted. Shoes, books, pencils. She allowed them to eat in bed if they wanted to and, of course, the children did want to.

Their mother liked frightening them, Gem and Anthony. She made herself hideous by cutting out long green teeth from plantain skin and sticking it over her own teeth, wrapping herself from head to toe in a sheet and covering her whole face with white powder. Then she would call the children.

Laughing, almost hysterically, they would run from her, she chasing behind them. Only when she saw they were truly afraid did she pull off the sheet and teeth, saying to the children, 'Don't be stupid. Look, it's your own Mummy.'

At Highdam people visited Clara all the time. Sometimes from the side of his platform window Archie could catch a glimpse of a dress tail disappearing up his backsteps. And when the wind blew he got a whiff of the provoking gales of kitchen laughter.

But the thing that haunted Clara, the thing she couldn't understand, even years after leaving Highdam, was why Sister Bea had stopped coming.

Sweet little Sister Bea, nimble for all her years, her narrow behind arching the air, her shifting feet giving those unexpectedly quick stamps before moving back into the shuffling weaving dance that made her one of the best queh-queh dancers in Highdam. She was always there the night before a wedding, leading the slow-moving line of men and women to the folk song sounds:

'Gooh nite aye, Gooh nite O
Ahwe cum-cum tell yuh Gooh nite'

Clara had been drawn to her ever since their first meeting at Doreen's queh-queh and the two of them struck up their own olderwoman-youngerwoman friendship. At the time Sister Bea lived by herself in the hut at the end of Long Dam, making cassava bread and casareep which she took to market some days. In those first few years of the Walcotts' moving to Highdam, Sister Bea dropped in each day to see Clara. Even if she only came out to get a bucket of water from the roadside pipe, she would come in, refreshing herself with a glass of lime drink, and on her market days she'd drop in some of the sweet cassava cake she hadn't sold that day.

Then when Anthony was a baby, just nine months old, abruptly she stopped coming. It was the day when Clara, with much guilt and even a feeling of betrayal, tied a piece of sickly smelling asafoetida around her baby's neck and dressed him in a blue nightdress as Rose had instructed. Anthony had been losing weight ever since he turned to greet his eighth month, and he was such a healthy baby. If ever there was a glowing looking child it was Anthony, his brown chubby arms, cuddling out of his sunsuit, Joe Louis arms, as his mother liked to say fondly. Clara breastfed him as she had done with her other two children, and also fed him porridge made from freshly grated green plantains. Bida, the East Indian woman from a neighbouring village, came and made a black spot between his brows to prevent people from giving him bad-eye and the child was fine. Then suddenly he began the dropping-off.

Clara let the first three weeks slip by and when she couldn't see any improvement, couldn't see any picking-back-up, she went to stick up a white flag at the side of the road to call in the doctor who came to the village only twice a week.

The doctor couldn't find anything wrong with the child and told Clara not to worry too much, he would pick up.

But Anthony, to his mother's mind, was getting worse, even his bright eyes seemed to be sinking in.

Then one day Rose came across while Sister Bea was there. As soon as Sister Bea left, Rose turned to Clara and, looking her full in the face, said in a calm voice, 'That woman that just gone there. That woman who in yuh house everyday. That woman responsible fuh yuh baby sickness. That woman is ole higue. I suspect it a long time.'

A rash of goose pimples spread across Clara's back and down her arms. 'What you talking about Rose?' she asked in pretended lightness.

'What I talking bout?' countered Rose who wasn't fooled by her innocence. 'What I talking bout?' she repeated with an enigmatic smile that wasn't a smile at all, just an upward move of her lips reserved for her own recognition of the supernatural forces at work.

'You know I don't believe in all dem things, Rose,' said Clara, going deeper into creole, as she did whenever she was a bit agitated. 'Dat is just ole talk. Ole higue changing they skin and ball-a-fire. You believe in all ah dat . . .' her voice petered out.

'I ain't talking bout no ball-a-fire,' said Rose. 'I talking bout people who keep they evil under calabash and use it to flourish on other people. You think everybody in the world like you? Sometimes people envy you fuh dat very reason. Why you think dat woman choose to live all by herself on Long Dam?'

Clara didn't answer.

Rose's eyes rested on her and there was nothing else to do but succumb to the knowing conviction she saw there.

Moving like a woman with a mission, Rose caught the old country bus that very afternoon and went down to the Mahaica Market. She came back with a cheap blue baby nightdress and some small brown balls of asafoetida in a brown paperbag. 'Ah bet you dat woman don't set foot back in this house,' she predicted.

The next day when Sister Bea visited she didn't stay long

and didn't even seem to glance into the corner where Anthony lay on the floor, curled on his side in a blue nightdress, a small ball of asafoetida hanging from a string around his neck like a crucifix.

All the same, as Rose predicted, from that day her feet never crossed the Walcotts' front or back door again, not once in the three years before she left to live with her brother in another village along the coast.

Instead she would call as she passed the house, 'How-dee, family,' and Clara would look out the window and say, 'How-dee, Sister Bea.' But their eyes hardly ever made four like before, and Clara felt torn by the hurt she thought she glimpsed in Sister Bea's eyes. At times she felt as if she was the one who had wronged.

When she told Rose, Rose only sucked her teeth and said, 'You too wishful.' And Clara consoled herself on one of her mother's sayings – 'there is more mystery between heaven and hell', or something like that.

But Dee-Dee kept coming, all through those years, amazing everyone with her energy. Walking all the way from Content to Highdam, walking slowly but assuredly, her face carrying the look of those who have arrived at the end of a long hard life.

She sat with her dry, cracked brown feet crossed on the front verandah, gently sucking on her tobacco pipe. Nearly seventy years ago she and her husband had come from India to work as indentured immigrants on the sugar estates. Her husband was long since dead and her sons and daughters were grown-up men and women with their own children. Still, it seemed that the desire to see India again had never left her.

Clara teased her gently about it. 'But Dee-Dee,' she would say, 'you have all your children and grandchildren here. Why you want to go back to India, eh? What so special about this India? Why it must haunt you so?'

Dee-Dee would go on chewing her pipe for a long time,

as if she had no intention of answering, and when her voice eventually came it was low and cracked, 'India, India . . .'

It was as if India was a big bright bubble, just out of reach, disappearing into nothingness whenever she tried to touch it.

Standing in sunlight water and watching the dark moving shapes of the fish below.

Standing with your fishing rod at the edge of a dam, waiting for the cork to duck, then jumping like mad after catching a small patwa.

Going to the backdam.

Rowing with Dinah in Uncle Joe boat, past the courida trees with their bird eggs. Some white and round, some more long and blueish.

Sitting on a box watching Cousin Nel peel off the thick coconut husk from the dry coconuts, breaking the coconuts and throwing them in a heap for copra, but passing you any of the sweet crunchy growie nuts she come across inside.

Things you'll miss about Highdam.

4

Election year, 1960. The last year for the Walcotts at Highdam, the year of Archie's retirement. The red-bricked public road stretching as far as Skeldon on the Corentyne, taking prospecting politicians up and down the coast. Election vans bumping along the road through rain and shine, and the voices coming through the loudspeakers, always slow and harsh and grating.

The Highdam people were surprised at the frequency with which it was announced that Mohabir was holding meetings along the upper East Coast. Rose always sucked her teeth when she heard that the Premier was going to speak that side. 'What he going that side for' she wanted to know, 'when the coolie like putty in he hand already?'

As in the previous elections, Archie could feel the tensions: the East Indians talking about everything else except politics, keeping that for when they were among themselves. And the black people talking hostile, some of them even a little bitter because they could see Mohabir coming to power again, and what could they expect from a coolie Premier? Nothing. Coolie was for coolie when all was said and done. Aphan Jhaat. Aphan Jhaat. He had nothing to give them.

And everyone knew that the fight was really between Mohabir's party, The National Labour Party – the NLP – and the People's Independent Party – the PIP – headed by the black leader, Atwell. Ferreira, the Portuguese man, heading the National United Front, had the votes of the big shots and middle-class coloured people, including the rich East Indian businessmen, but all of these supporters made up only a handful of the population so he didn't stand a chance. The other parties that had mushroomed in the last year were only monkeying around. 'Plenty monkey politics,' the people thought.

Lionel's party came under the monkey brand. Lionel, Archie's second or third cousin, had inaugurated his own party a few months back, the Nation's Independent Party, and in conversation Lionel referred to it as NIP.

Short and trim with a winning smile and agile mind, Lionel's unfailing enthusiasm irritated a lot of people who thought he had gotten away without the usual bouts of despair and depression that seem to plague most people all their lives. He always left his cousin Archie feeling very tired.

From as far back as Archie could remember, Lionel was forever into some new venture or other. He had tried his hand at pork-knocking when he was younger, joining an expedition of rough-tough men, pushing through the heart of the Guiana jungle in search of gold. But he returned to the city two months later with severe bat bites and stories of how the other pork-knockers had tried to drown him when they were crossing the rapids. What happened in actual fact was that the city-bred Lionel was petrified at the idea of leaving the boat to join the men in pushing it over the rocks and out of the relentlessly swirling water. In the end, seeing that he had turned to stone, the other men got out to manoeuvre the boat as best they could safely over the rapids. For those timeless moments when he was tossed, soaked and battered from one side of the boat to the other, Lionel must have thought the men were really out to drown

31

him. And the thing that amazed his friends was how they had managed to resist.

Archie didn't have any sympathy to give him when he returned from the expedition without any gold to show. But he did allow him to spend the week recovering as he looked in a really bad way. During this week Lionel managed to persuade Clara, who didn't need much persuading, that he knew how to make soap. Intrigued by his inventiveness, she gave him two of her largest saucepans, coconut oil, a pound of caustic soda, among other things, and stood back to watch the operation. The results were two rock-hard cakes of bright yellow soap which she never used for fear of burning her hands and two pots that had turned into brown-stained sieves.

After the pork-knocking Lionel had tried his hand at many things, giving them up as soon as his interest began to wane. Finally he settled on being a poultry rearer on a farm along the East Coast, with the indispensable help of his brother. Archie had considered it the first wise move he had made in his life. Now Lionel was a politician.

It was this new forty-five-year-old Lionel, his unruly hair brushed back with brilliantine, his familiar skin-teeth smile, who came to ask Archie if he would consider standing as a candidate for NIP. 'NIP stands a very good chance,' he asserted, 'a very good chance, man. We have some influential people backing the party, the Coopers from Bartica, diamond dealers, well-known up and down the country. The Richards from New Amsterdam, son of Dr Richards and the Chans who own the big supermarket at McKenzie. Give it a chance.'

Archie's face wasn't given to smiling or laughing that often. But he had to laugh, his face going into a grin, pulling the tight muscles across his cheekbones, making him look years younger and, in a funny way, like a chortling old man.

'You have to be joking, man,' he said, still grinning, 'I don't have that kind of interest in politics, boy. You're always with these brainwaves. Who tell you I'm interested in becoming politician?' Archie put a hand to his forehead and gently began to massage the space between his brows, a sign that he was suffering from one of his headaches. 'You know I have this sinus trouble, boy, and you're asking me about what, candidate? Every day, three four times a day, I have to take aspirins.'

But in spite of himself he was curious to know what Lionel's party stood for. 'Basically about self-government and a better way of life for the people,' said Lionel, launching into his party manifesto. 'But we wouldn't go for independence in a hurry. The country must be able to handle itself first. Man, they have a lot of people who don't like this government.'

Archie had started to grin again but he sobered up when Lionel asked if he couldn't help with some 'finance' to print more party leaflets.

Archie, of course, had no money give. He found it truly amazing that Lionel was really serious about his shot-gun party and even entertained hopes of winning a few seats.

'The man is a real simpleton,' he said to Clara afterwards.

About a week before the election Ferreira surprised the people of Highdam by announcing a meeting to be held in front of the school. He hadn't done much campaigning in the rural areas, but in the frenzy of the last minute election bid he, like the other politicians, was campaigning left, right and centre.

On the afternoon of the meeting a van drove up to the school and four men began to erect a makeshift platform with a speaker. The children, going home from school, crowded around to watch and only moved off when Archie came out with his wild cane. This first Highdam meeting had aroused everybody's curiosity, even though the news was greeted with many suck-teeths. Just as dusk was beginning to fall and the mosquitoes and sandflies to come out,

33

Ferreira and his black candidate for the Lower East Coast area drove up in a cloud of red dust, followed by an NUF jeep.

The meeting was turning out to be bigger than Archie expected. People kept coming, including the East Indians from the surrounding villages. The Highdam people walked with their smoke-pots to ward off the mosquitoes and sandflies, swinging them round and round and sending off showers of tiny sparks.

Ferreira and his candidate sat at the front on the chairs they had brought. Ferreira, sitting with his legs folded, did his best not to fidget or scratch, but his candidate, a dark, big bellied man couldn't help slapping the annoying insects from his face, even as he mounted the platform with a brisk reluctance. Just before he reached the microphone, a man darted in front of him to test it again, shouting, 'Testing testing one two one two,' sending the crowd into laughter. My people, thought Archie, my people, anything for a laugh, though he himself joined in.

The candidate for the Lower East Coast was an ex-farmer and Ferreira thought this should make people feel some kind of kinship with him. But someone in the crowd called out 'black stooge' the moment the candidate took to the mike. Seemingly unperturbed, he launched into a fiery speech about the vital role of farmers. Ferreira rewarded him with a little smile at the end, but the candidate's cheeks still trembled with indignation as he stepped down from the platform.

Archie straightened up slightly, preparing himself for Ferreira, even though he was fully acquainted with his stand: Ferreira did not believe in revolution but in reform; Ferreira did not believe in nationalisation but in private investment; Ferreira was in no hurry to see the country gain independence. Archie didn't have any choice but to give this man his vote. He thought Ferreira was a sound man with sensible plans for the country, not rash like Mohabir or Atwell. Like Ferreira, he didn't think that Guiana was at all ready for independence. To cut itself off from the apron strings of the British was to leave the way open for the Russians to walk in.

Ferreira, tall and thin, smoothed back his hair and paused before the microphone, bracing himself for a lengthy speech. His first words were, 'In a week from now, my friends, you go to the polls.'

In a low, earnest voice, he wasted no time in warning of the things to come if Mohabir was re-elected. 'Today, my friends, it is your money and properties which the government is after,' he said simply. 'Tomorrow it will be your very freedom. Already we suffer before elections. Just think, what will be our lot if the present party in power wins? Then there is all the talk about independence. Can you imagine independence under such a government? I believe that independence is a necessary goal for all colonies, but at the same time let us be realistic, my friends. Independence carries grave responsibilities. Responsibilities which I feel we're not equipped to carry as yet. Independence will come but we must crawl before we can walk. Right now I am more interested in pulling the country out of its present economic stagnation by encouraging private investment to boost the economy; by giving loans to farmers to fully develop and exploit our rich resources . . .'

At the reference to farmers, some Highdam listeners began to snigger, and one man cried out, 'Fancy talk, fancy talk!'

'My party is fully aware of the problems that farmers face,' Ferreira went on, 'but let me say this – I do not believe in revolution. I believe in reform, the slow and steady pace of development which is the highway to happiness in the long run. My friends, I can say no more, I can only exhort you to vote wisely when you cast your ballot on July the third. I can only ask you to vote National United Front.'

As the meeting broke up and people began to drift away, an anti-communist leaflet was thrust into Archie's hand by one of Ferreira's supporters who had been distributing them to the crowd.

On election day, there was a ceaseless interplay of rain falling and sun shining, the kind of weather that made children run around chanting, 'Devil and he wife fighting'. The Highdam school which was used as a polling station was damp and full of mosquitoes. The voters, a lot of them East Indians from the surrounding villages, stood patiently, one behind the other, and allowed their fingers to be dipped in red stain afterwards as proof that they had exercised the franchise.

That evening the ears of the nation were glued to radios as people in their homes, in rumshops and cakeshops, tuned in to the incoming election results. Men knocked back shots of rum and placed bets as to who would win. Archie and Clara stayed up late and Rose brought across some roast corn to mark the occasion. By eleven o'clock it was pretty clear that Mohabir was sweeping the polls. Results from the remote savannah areas were still to come in, and even though Archie knew that Ferreira had a strong hold of Amerindian votes in these districts, he also knew that the party of his choice hadn't the faintest hope. 'Atwell dead. Ferreira done bury,' the voice of someone drunk called out into the night.

'Well, I think I'll call it a night folks,' said Archie, getting up from his Berbice chair. 'Looks like we're in for another spell of Mohabir.'

'Night-Night, Teach,' said Rose, as Archie retired for the night.

On the following day, carloads and truckloads of East Indians stormed the city to celebrate Mohabir's victory. Archie was taken aback by what he considered this brazen display of triumph and power, open trucks filled with dancing, drumming people, moving down to the city. Dangerously overloaded cars, tooting horns in wedding-like spirits, dragged behind them in the dust noisy tin cans and the ends of old mops, the mop being the symbol of Atwell's party. Of course there were clashes between the victorious and defeated sides.

Amidst the election aftermath and the hysteria that Cuba was generating in the local and foreign news, the Walcotts prepared to leave Highdam. The children who had always known that they would move to the city when their father retired, seemed to be taking it all in their stride.

Archie was taking his retirement a year early, as advised by his doctor, and his pension wasn't going to be affected in any way. He had been looking around for a house to buy in Georgetown for some time and had eventually found one. Clara went down to see it and told the children all about the new flush toilet they'd be using and the sink with real running water from the taps. 'No more pit latrines or fetching water from the standpipe,' she enthused to the children, describing in detail the new conveniences, the overhead tank in the toilet, the ball and chain.

Weeks before the family moved, people kept coming to discuss the new life ahead of them and to help with the clearing and packing up. 'Don't forget to throw the white rum in the corners of the new house,' Rose told Clara, 'to purge it out and get rid of the bad spirits.'

But it wasn't without regrets or misgivings that Archie was leaving Highdam. He would miss his long country walks, the fresh cow's milk, the air and even the people. Still, he told himself, the move was best for the sake of his children, to have them, now that they were growing older, in a more progressive atmosphere.

On the very day of leaving, Clara's big brown and white cat gave birth to three kittens, and devoured them almost immediately. Clara, who couldn't bear to look at the cat, told Aunt May that she could keep her. Clara and Rose held each other tightly and cried.

Georgetown. Magic in the street lights, money everywhere, people everywhere, walking up and down the pavements eating nuts, channa, ice-cream cones, popcorn. Flamboyant trees shedding red petals in the avenues. On Friday nights women selling gleaming coils of black pudding at the street corners in little carts.

Georgetown. Stabroek Market with the big clock. The dim crowded rumshops, ten alone you count on Camp Street, and the voices from them, not voices at all, but words, just words jumble up together.

You press your mother into letting you run every little errand just for the chance to walk down those streets.

You keep going back to Norton – the one with the fountain. Not the side full of rusty cars, broken down houses and the funeral parlour, but the part with the blue and white cafe and the marble fountain, the water curving in an arc into the air, then falling like fine rain into a pool below.

On Sunday afternoons you, Dinah, your mother and Anthony go down to the sea wall. Your mother played here as a girl, running around on the sandy beach below, wading in the water, watching the waves bring in shoals of little four-eye fish and taking them back out again. One day, she said, she and her cousin were playing on the beach. They could see the skies getting darker and knew a rainstorm was coming but still they stayed. It took the first peel of thunder to send them running home because it felt just as if the whole Atlantic was opening to swallow them up.

Your mother tell you and Anthony to be careful when you play on the beach, especially around the jetty, because the currents take some children out to sea for good.

You walk past the Round House with the militia band playing and you could see the lighthouse, a tall tall red-and-white striped building. You find a few dead four-eye fish washed up on the shore.

5

No one knew how much unease the sight of his Georgetown house caused him. A simple white house, oblong in
shape, with a roof slanting downwards from front to back, it
was on the southern side of Princess Street. The breezy side
that he liked was paled by a fence of brown paling staves. It
was a house with many windows, giving it a well-ventilated
appearance, and it stood on long wooden pillars like so
many of the other houses. The house had two bedrooms,
fairly large, and two flights of stairs, back and front. The
doors and bannisters were painted in rust-red and there was
ample yard space. There was a small coconut palm at the
front of the yard and a flowering shrub bearing tiny purple
flowers that fell easily in the wind. In the back garden stood
a slim, white-trunked gooseberry tree and Archie himself
had planted things like bora, ochroes and tomatoes.

The house, which was only three doors away from the
busy Camp and Princess Street junction, gave the appearance of being quiet and aloof. Archie had been taken in by
this serenity at first. During his last few months at Highdam
he had visited it on several occasions before finally making
the purchase from an East Indian businessman.

He had weighed the pros and cons carefully and, taking

all things into consideration, decided that it was a reasonable bargain – it was new, had sufficient yard space, was on the cool side of the street, in a central position and cost ten thousand dollars. Apart from these factors which he considered essential, especially the yard space, the general harassment of house hunting had worn down his fastidiousness so that even when he had discovered flaws in the setting, Princess Street was still bought.

One of the major flaws that had given him disquiet was the open tenement yard behind his house. On the first occasion he had seen it he was jolted. The front view of his home gave no indication of its existence. To be greeted from his back window by the sight of tumbledown buildings and range rooms all huddled together, and a teeming humanity, was both unpleasant and disturbing. This blending of contrast in Georgetown, of the old and dilapidated beside the new and elegant, never ceased to amaze him.

After the initial shock had waned he began his practical reasoning again. Obviously the place was not as quiet as he had imagined, though Princess Street itself was much quieter than Camp and had an almost residential appearance. His yard was also paled, he reasoned, and behind that paling was a passageway, about eight feet wide, separating him from the tenement. This layout, he felt, would give him some measure of protection and he also recognised that he would never be able to find a place that would suit him in every way.

In less than a week after the family had moved in, Archie knew the full extent of his lot. The passageway and his paling were fragile barriers to the shouting, laughing and cursing next door. The mingling scents of cooking, the clanking of buckets at the standpipe and the dukebox music that was played at any hour, all took on a dull permanence. Apart from this, the corner rumshop which had seemed a good way off in the beginning was really too close for comfort. It unapologetically issued forth the latest calypsoes and other music far into the night.

The rumshop was owned by the Ramsammys who lived above it. They also owned the three small unpainted houses in the tenement yard; ramshackle rooms bracing each other for support; the numerous cubby holes on the other side of the rumshop; the yard toilet and roofless zinc bathroom shared by nearly twenty families.

In the farthest corner of this Charlestown kingdom lived Mr Percy and his lady, Miss Sheila. What a combination! Gem thought Miss Sheila a beautiful woman. She could tell that everyone in the yard thought so too, the way they watched whenever she passed by, which wasn't often. A well-built, dark-skinned woman in her mid-thirties, Miss Sheila held her plump ebony neck with grace, and even from the window of her small unpainted house, anyone could see that she was always well-dressed.

Miss Sheila, who was polite and always had a smile for everyone, hardly ever left the house, and to Gem she seemed like an African queen committed, for some reason or other, to spending her life in the Charlestown yard.

The man she lived with, Mr Percy, was a renowned and hardened criminal and everyone in the yard regarded him with awe and fear. He was a tall, muscular man but his entire face and neck had been ruined by acid so that it looked as if a thin plastic skin had been pulled tightly over his face, flattening his nose and cheekbones and leaving tiny puckers on his features.

Mr Percy moved about the yard in a silent, sinister manner and for some reason or other the only person he ever said anything to was Mr Walcott. Whenever he happened to see him from across the paling he always said good morning.

Rumour had it in the yard that it was Miss Sheila who threw the acid on him and then went over to America to live. She didn't stay long, though, and when she came back she took up living with Mr Percy, never going any place and acting as if she lived only for him. People said that Mr

Percy must have done something to bring her back and that she couldn't leave him even if she wanted to because he had worked obeah on her.

Then there was Mrs Payne with her six children in one of the three small houses, and just a door away from her was Mrs Lall, the only East Indian person living in the open yard. Everybody expected her to tread easily among the black people, but as it was she was a peppery woman, prone to prolong any incident by talking about it in a whining voice hours after everybody else had cooled down.

Mrs Lall's thin mouth was in a perpetual sneer as she moved her short, heavy frame between the Charlestown yard and her stall in La Penitence Market, her grey-streaked hair dangling in a fat plait behind her. Mrs Lall's fetish about keeping her house clean and scrubbing and shifting her furniture late at night had earned her the reputation of being 'haunted'. People felt that she must have murdered her pandit husband, Mishri, who had died a natural death four years ago.

Then there was Mr Castello. Mr Castello lived with his wife, who was blind, in a tiny cottage to the side of the Walcotts' front entrance. He bought things like old stoves, chairs, tables and lamps, then he fixed them up with paint and sold them again. He was a small, grey-headed man in his mid-sixties and exuded an air of reckless violence. He drank a lot and his large, grey eyes were nearly always bloodshot. Mr Castello stammered slightly and when enraged his head shook uncontrollably.

Clara allowed Gem to run errands for his wife, a dark, soft-spoken woman whom Mr Castello, in his sober moments, took on his arm for a walk.

Gem discovered that Mr Castello became very irritable if people told him 'good morning' or 'good afternoon' more than was necessary and, unknown to her parents, she sometimes passed his way deliberately, up and down, each time telling him a good morning.

'Good morning, Master Castello,' she would say, her face

just over his wooden gate, wearing a smile as if nothing else in the world mattered more than saying good morning. And Mr Castello, bending over some stove or other, would glance up at her with his large bloodshot eyes and mutter 'good morning'. Two minutes later Gem would pass back again, repeating the greeting: 'Good morning, Master Castello,' her tongue relishing the use of the word 'Master'.

Usually Mr Castello answered up to the third good morning. The fourth he ignored. Any good morning after that was to ask for the wrath of God. He would rise up slowly, his head shaking as if he were about to have a fit: 'Good morning, scunt! Good morning, rass!' he'd scream. 'Why de rass you don't tell yuh mother rass good morning?'

As these words Gem and Anthony would double up with laughter under the house and Clara would wonder who it was that Mr Castello was cursing.

Apart from this, hardly a day passed without a beating or a quarrel in the Charlestown yard. Mrs Payne and Mrs Lall were deadly enemies. Mrs Payne's daily threat to her was: 'If I put mih hand on you, I get trouble fuh you.'

At other times she said, 'Coolie people suh nasty. All that scrubbing and scrubbing you going on with as if you suh clean and the next minute you hawking in you kitchen sink. Coolie people really nasty, ah tell you.'

To which Mrs Lall would reply in her high nasal voice: 'Eh heh, eh heh, is nastiness mek we progress in the world so. Eh heh, me ah Pandit Mishri wife and me nasty.'

'Pandit wife! Pandit wife!' Mrs Payne would exclaim, mimicking her in a high voice, 'you kill de poor man and calling yourself Pandit wife.'

'Eh heh, eh heh, you beena dey when I kill he. Is de two ahwe kill he. Na true, na true? But me get all de money an you na get none, that's why you so vex in you spirit.'

'Kyak kyak kyak,' Mrs Payne would laugh, 'but hear this ole bitch. I vex in me spirit! Ah mad come an put a cuff in you.'

'Come na. Come na. Ah gat this cutlish waiting fuh you. Me na gat nobody to defend me, you know. Eh heh, eh heh. Me only gat this cutlish to defend me.'

Suddenly Mrs Payne would turn on her dukebox full blast to drown out the whining voice, and Mrs Lall, her face swollen with rage, would begin beating an old tin drum heavily, screaming out at the top of her lungs, 'You tink is only you kyan mek noise. You tink is only you kyan mek noise.'

One day Mrs Lall had spied Dinah, Gem and Clara out walking and had hurried across to meet them.

'Owh nabe, you don't know how much I love black people,' she admitted as if she'd been dying to get this off her chest for the longest while. 'I really love dose people, na tink seh because I does quarrel pan them I don't like them. I love black people to my heart. I really love dose people.'

Dinah gave a little snigger of disbelief while Clara quelled her with an eye and said, 'I know nabe, but youall must try to take things easy. Try not to quarrel too much.'

'Owh nabe,' she said, shaking her head, then changed the subject abruptly to politics, picking on Premier Mohabir. 'Owh nabe, but ah what dat man doing to ahwee dese na, all dis taxation an dat taxation. He ah really treat ahwee dese bad.' She looked at them imploringly.

As soon as they had moved off, Dinah laughed and sucked her teeth. 'But is why East Indian people like to lie so? You can just look at her face and see she lying. I love black people! And pretending she don't like Mohabir.'

It was Jeannette, the youngest of Mrs Payne's brood, who really brought about the gradual integration of the Walcotts into the yard.

Jeanette, a thin wiry child of about six, stole her mother's five-cent piece and swore to the bitter end that she hadn't, preferring to suffer almost anything rather than to hand it over, strengthened by the knowledge that she would be able to spend it in some quiet moment.

Mrs Payne, struggling to make ends meet, usually caught her between her huge thighs and squeezed her. At other times she grabbed her and lashed her against the ground. One day she even forced her into a rice bag, held the top, and sent one of the older children to get the matches, pretending she was going to set her alight.

Clara, who could no longer bear the hoarse, terrified screams of the child, opened her back window and leaned out. She had witnessed the entire scene and had turned to her husband, trembling: 'This is sheer madness, Archie, one of these days she's going to kill that child.'

Then she heard her own voice pleading: 'Mrs Payne, Mrs Payne, that is enough, please let her go. Mrs Payne, that is enough.'

Mrs Payne looked surprised. She released the mouth of the bag, panting heavily, 'Missis Walcott you don't know this little girl here, you don't know this little girl here, ah tell yuh, this Jeanette here,' she said, putting some final shakes in Jeanette who looked like a small wild sensa fowl, ready to dash off at the first opportunity.

But Clara's plea seemed to have worked, for the very next day Mrs Payne sent over a bowl of black pudding with Jeanette. Clara accepted it and afterwards she told Mrs Payne, from the side window, how nice it tasted.

When she came back into the bedroom Archie said 'Aieee' in a suffering kind of way. 'I suppose you know what you're doing. This is their way of trying to get close.'

And he was right about the getting close for after that little Jeanette became like an addition to the family. Whenever her mother was about to beat her she ran across, bawling to the top of her voice, 'Owh Mrs Walcott, save me, save me.' In her frantic haste to escape she had already pulled out one of the paling staves in Archie's back gate.

'Look, open the door quick for that little mad woman,' Archie would urge as Jeanette brammed down the front door. 'Quick, before she breaks it down.'

Panting like a frightened little creature, Jeanette would

cling to Clara's waist, and after that her mother would lose all interest in her. She'd stay with the Walcotts for the rest of the day, sharing in the meals and doing the odd little things that Clara gave her to do.

One midday when Archie was slicing into a boiled yellow plantain, eating deftly with his knife and fork, she looked him full in the face and asked in a husky inquisitive voice, 'You eat with knife. You eat with fork. Wha mek you na eat with spoon?' The whole family burst out laughing, even Archie grinned, the muscles pulling back in his cheeks.

Two of Jeanette's older sisters, about Gem's and Anthony's ages, also began to come across to play. The thought did enter Archie's head that he should nail up the back gate but he knew that wouldn't solve anything. He had already seen the girls, as well as Gem, climbing over the paling.

What could he do when his own children behaved this way?

The Duke coming. The Duke of Edinburgh.

At school the teachers talk about the visit which is all because Guiana is part of the British Empire. You preferred if it was the Queen coming though, in her gown and crown.

Nearly every night your mother would take you and Anthony to see the lighting up all over Georgetown for the visit. All the flamboyant trees on Main Street Avenue full of electric bulbs, hanging like see-through pears of every shade from every tree, right and left of the avenue as far as your eye could see. St George's Cathedral which they say is the highest wooden building in the world is washed in floodlights, glowing tall and white as if someone had painted it in moonlight. The Town Hall looking like a lovely icing cake because it's so studded with lights. All the shops and stores bright with new lights too, the big ones and the small. Some flashing lights saying 'Welcome', others looking as if they're embroidered in lights. Only Chin grocery shop is dark.

But you're always going into Chin shop to buy fluties, sweet red-water ice blocks that turn your tongue bright pink. You'd go into Chin shop and wait patiently for him to come and sell you because his shop always full of people. People like his saltbeef and pigtail.

Chin flat, pale, smooth, always wearing a white singlet and short Khaki pants, his rubber slippers flapping up behind him. The back of the shop musty and dark, full of bags of rice and sugar piled one on top the other.

One day, a boy, a little bigger than you, come into Chin shop and begin to call for a long list of things; 'Twenty-four tin carnation milk, twelve cake soap, twelve pound sugar, four pound saltbeef, six tin tomato paste, six box match, six tin sardine, four pound cheese . . .'

From the look on his face you know he only joking. Chin must be stupid not to see that the boy only joking, that he don't have money to pay for all the things Chin busy heaping on the counter, walking up and down, weighing this and that, his slippers flapping.

You begin to giggle in anticipation. When Chin finish, the boy start to laugh too: 'Man, Chin, what wrong with you, man? You don't know is fun I making? Where I going get money to buy all them thing, man?'

A red flush spreading across Chin face and his eyes becoming even narrower. Chin looking now as if he's trying hard to control himself, smiling: 'Nice, nice lil boy, come give me hand a shake,' stretching out his hand across the counter.

'Don't put out yuh hand. Don't put out yuh hand, boy,' you say, still laughing. But the boy already putting out his hand into Chin hand uncertainly, not knowing whether Chin still vex or taking the whole thing as a joke. Chin grip the boy palm with his hand and begin to squeeze, squeezing and squeezing as if he want to crack every bone inside the boy hand.

But you still go into Chin shop, and another time when it was just you alone inside, Chin lean across the counter to pinch one of the small brown nipples just showing under your cotton dress. 'Eeeeh! You getting beeg,' he say.

The pinch hurt you and you hurry out of the shop, feeling Chin is a dirty old lizard.

You have to get new school uniform to march with the other schoolchildren to go and see the Duke. New yachting shoes, new socks, new navy blue kimona, new cream blouse, new beret. But you know your father won't give the money. That you'd be lucky to get anything new at all.

6

Archie walked briskly from the cool interior of the Public Free Library into the brilliantly hot afternoon. He was wearing his grey flannel trousers today, white shirt tucked neatly in his waist, his old leather briefcase carrying the two books he had just exchanged at the library, *Puck of Pook's Hill* by Kipling and a collection of short stories by Alberto Moravia.

He crossed over on to the busy shopping junction in front of Bookers' Stores and made his way round into Water Street. As he walked along the narrow crowded pavement a stream of traffic moved sluggishly along with him. Yellow buses, cars and wobbling pedal cyclists, trucks, horses, pulling long, over-laden dray carts, huge sugarbulks which left odd little trails of golden brown crystals on the streets behind. Sweet Demerara sugar, brown as the Demerara River.

Most of the shops and stores were closing early today because nearly everyone wanted to see the Duke or had given their employers that impression. Archie himself wanted to get a loaf of wholemeal bread and to pick up a lock for the little cupboard fitted into his writing desk before the shop closed.

The sunshine permeated everything, a thin hazy vapour seeming to rise from the hot asphalt streets and he welcomed the cooling breezes that the Atlantic kept pushing in. Georgetown was at its most teeming on this Friday four o'clock weekend afternoon with shoppers and workers pouring out of offices and factories and people drifting off to different assembly points to see the Duke.

Archie stopped at a small cakeshop to cool himself down on a glass of mauby and ice. As he sipped the slightly fermented barky drink, he watched the jostling move of people going by, a *mélange* of people of different races and different shades and mixtures of races. Africans, East Indians, Portuguese, Chinese, a few Amerindians and, of course, the growing numbers of Mixed. He watched the hustle of the pavement vendors fastening on to prospective buyers, selling anything from a safety pin to a bottle of Shiling oil, an all-purpose remedy for colds, toothache, sore-throats and a heap of other ailments. He eyed a couple of young men going up to people with their usual 'Give me a raise nuh, man,' in the hope of scrounging a few cents.

Archie walked on, chin slightly lifted, marvelling how the years had flown. This afternoon, for some reason, the memory of Highdam had invaded his senses. It was exactly eight months since he had left the village. Eight months since he had retired after contributing nearly forty years of dedicated service to the teaching profession.

Today, Highdam was coming back as a vision of rural purity, and suddenly he wasn't consoled by the fact that he had left it for the sake of his children. Maybe he should have realised that he was a countryman and that his spirit was best in the openness of space and land. He would never grow accustomed to the close proximity of the Georgetown houses. To the noise. The thieves. The hooligans. The slums. Not to mention the growing political tension which was obvious in spite of the lights, the streamers, the other outward signs of welcome for the Duke.

'Anti-Working Class Budget', 'No Independence Under

Mohabir', 'Budget of Sorrow', were some of the placards that caught Archie's eye as he passed groups of anti-government demonstrators who were seizing the opportunity of the royal visit to embarrass the government.

As he approached the corner that led to his Princess Street home, he became aware of the police detouring traffic; of the barricades and din of voices above the street; of the heaving mass of human bodies blocking off the corner for a glimpse of the Duke. Archie, who would not have gone out of his way to see the Duke, debated within himself whether he should try to approach his home from another angle. But this struck him as useless, or at best, too much trouble. He edged his way into the patchwork of bodies, and was immediately engulfed.

The sun had reduced its intensity a little but people were becoming restless. There was less laughing and more cursing. The police broke up a scuffle between a fat woman in a tight red dress and a wiry man, who had just 'grind me foot off,' as she put it.

Unmindful of the cantering white horses, barricades and restraining teachers, school children, carrying little replicas of the British flag, squeezed their way through to get to the shave-ice cart installed in front of the rumshop. The shave-ice man, hot and bothered by the growing cluster of children around him, shaved frantically, scooping the crushed ice out with his hand, dipping it quickly into one or two of his thick coloured syrups, and passing it to the crowd of children without looking. Working as much out of greed for the coins thrust under his nose as for the desire to get rid of them, his hands moved non-stop. But still the children cried, 'Mister, Mister, a shave ice. Look Mister, I standing up hey before she. Mister, Mister, a shave ice.'

Archie clutched his briefcase in the crowd. He knew that it wasn't so much the Duke as the thirst for spectacle and drama that had brought people out in the thousands.

One of the picketers, a thin-chested man, held his 'Budget of Sorrow' in a careless manner. The stiff card-board picket grazed the cheek of a man in front.

'Mind how you holding you picket,' the man warned, as he pushed the placard aside, but the picketer was too occupied with himself and picket to take note.

'Ah say, mind how you holding you damn placard, man. All-you fanaticals don't look wha all-you doing.'

Further down a young policeman was having a hard time keeping the crowd from pushing down one of the barricades. He warned the pushers at the back and they began to taunt him mercilessly. 'You ugly son-of-a-bitch,' a youth bawled out from behind.

'You ignorant,' the policeman answered back.

'Is only the Police Force would tek all like you,' another voice taunted.

'I have the education up here,' said the policeman, pointing to his white cap. 'I have five subjects GCE and could get anywhere. The only place you got to go is lot 12,' Lot 12 being another name for the Georgetown jail.

But the people had already erupted into loud derisive laughter. 'Five subjects GCE, eh!eh! look at Mister-Five Subjects-GCE.'

'Thank the Lord I only have me little ten-subjects-at-two-sittings,' exclaimed a middle-aged woman mockingly, pressing her hands to her two ample breasts. Above the laughter a siren was heard in the distance. A white police car flashed by.

Word passed around that the Duke had reached the head of the city, and the crowd, injected with new vigour, heard the unmistakeable muffled roar of the police outriders.

Slowly the outriders came into view, ebony faces covered in beads of perspiration, sitting painfully erect on two huge, droning white motorbikes.

School children waved their red, white and blue flags crazily, picketers thrust forward their placards, the whole crowd craning forward at the sight of the long, elegant black car bearing the Duke.

In spite of being hemmed in, Archie caught a glimpse of

54

the white figure in close-fitting tunic, moving his hand from left to right.

'Eh, eh, but he look just like the picture on the almanac, eh?' one woman observed to another. 'Ah wonder if he does wear dem clothes all the time?'

'Man, watch de red, white and blue pon de shoulder,' said the other one.

Beside the Duke sat Governor Rothschild, taking refuge behind light-green sun glasses, his European eyes still unadjusted to the harsh light after three years in the tropics.

It was the sudden wave of boos that alerted Archie to the passing of the Premier and his wife, and shouts of 'Mohabir resign'. From behind the closed windows of their small grey car, the Premier, a good-looking man in his late forties, endured the boos with a resigned smile while his wife held up two defiant fingers in a victory sign. Georgetown certainly wasn't their stronghold.

At that moment Archie felt a hand slipping from his back pocket. His own hand shot around in quick protective reflex, but too late, his bicycle key, ball-point pen and a couple of coins were gone. Luckily he kept little or no money in his back pocket.

Archie was borne away by the sea of human bodies towards his home. He stopped for a few moments on the parapet to allow the crowds to lighten, then turned into his gateway. Just then the wind brought a fine spray of unexpected rain to his face.

Marching in your new white yachting shoes and white socks, the only new things you get for the Duke. Marching till your foot get a blister. Waiting and waiting in the hot sun at the Parade Ground. Waiting for the chance to wave your little red, blue and white flag. Then the siren noise and stirring and the Duke coming. Looking like the picture on your exercise book cover. The one with he and the queen together. Everybody waving flags. Afterwards going back to school to get a pepsi and sweetbread. Afterwards taking off your shoes and socks and walking home barefoot. Hearing your father say, maybe it wasn't the best thing moving to Georgetown after all.

7

Strings of lights still showed all that was beautiful in Georgetown and people still gathered in smaller numbers to see him wherever he passed. But for the remainder of the Duke's visit the expectancy, the vibrancy was gone, replaced by a quieter waiting restlessness.

It was there in the eyes of the limers, young men who couldn't find work or who perhaps didn't want to find work, lounging around the street corners, making soft obscene promises to the women going by, 'Girl, if I only get you . . .'

It was there, as usual, in the eyes of the half-naked, under-nourished, bewildered children, standing in the dark doorways of the Albouystown shacks. There in the eyes of the prostitutes on Lombard Street, cursing under their breath and leaning against time. In the eyes of the steve-dores, working through the steamy mornings. In the tired smiles of the shop and factory girls at the end of a day.

Down at the Ministry of Culture where Dinah Walcott worked, it was there too, but overridden by an all pervasive boredom.

At nineteen, Dinah thought herself to be bright, lucky and nice to look at. And she was all three, coolly taking everything in her stride, amazing her mother who had slipped into marriage like a duck into the inevitable waters of life. What else was there to do in her time?

Within a month of moving to the city Dinah, against Archie's wishes, gave up her teaching career and three weeks later got herself a job in no less a place than the Civil Service. She was an Assistant Officer in the Publications department of the Ministry of Culture.

Everyone was surprised at the ease with which she got the job since it wasn't in keeping with the feeling of the Georgetown black people that the government was taking on only their own 'coolie'. Dinah was given a test, summoned for an interview and within a week was working in her new job which included proof-reading material before it was published, among other things.

'My daughter is going to be somebody,' said Clara.

Archie remained silent. Ever since she had given up her teacher job he had developed this silence about her activities, a silence that acknowledged she had slipped beyond his control. Teaching was a hard but safe profession; now she was directly under the influence of a government with communist leanings.

But he needn't have worried. Apart from the new Minister of Culture himself and his Permanent Secretary, who were nearly always out of the building, the Ministry, like the rest of the Civil Service was overwhelmingly anti-Mohabir.

Dinah rode her bicycle every day into the sprawling sandy yard of the Ministry where drivers, waiting for their assignments, lolled against government landrovers and other vehicles, eyeing her smooth brown legs slyly.

Her office was one of those former colonial mansions, converted into the Ministry only by the wooden plaque at its front. Its cool green and white exterior, its many jalousies and verandahs said more about the ability of the British to provide for themselves in the tropics than the efficient layout of a government ministry. The various departments were all functioning in what were previously bedrooms, living rooms, dining halls and kitchens and perhaps this contributed to its disjointed functioning.

Workers from the Accounts division, too lazy to come downstairs, lowered their files and papers to the division below in a basket attached to a rope through the open window.

Inside the building civil servants leaned or sat on the edge of each other's desks, discussing the demonstration that was being called by the Civil Service Association for a wage increase; discussing the budget; how things were hard in the country; how Mohabir was putting his people into top positions; the latest films at the cinemas.

In the Publications department only a young, sleek-haired East Indian messenger was busy, operating an old Gestetner machine, his shoulders bent from trying to please everybody, his eyes resentful.

A short Portuguese typist was talking about the coming march to two of her colleagues, 'I don't think I able with no march child, not in dat hot sun. When I get peely-peely and me husband leave me, trade union can't help me. I en able get sunstroke fuh couple dollars more.'

'Well I marching,' said the taller brownskin, Mrs Steward, 'I damn fed up with the situation in this country. You too blasted lazy,' she added hotly, turning to the Portuguese typist. 'You want to sit back and enjoy the sweetness when it come. Is five years now I working in this place and can't get a promotion. This country don't have no future. I glad let me daughter mekhaste and get out a dis place.'

'Whey she going?' inquired another thin young coloured girl by the name of Miss De Young. She had heard it all before but still maintained an insatiable curiosity.

'To 'merica,' said Mrs Steward casually. 'She leaving next month. All me family in the States now, you know.'

Miss De Young knew, but still pressed, 'So when you going join she?'

'Who me? Another year or two. I want all me papers fix up. I ent want go on no holiday. Me sister glad to get me over there.'

'She like the place?' went on Miss De Young.

'She must like the place,' said Mrs Steward indignantly. Then remembering something she added, 'Wait, I din show you the last set a pictures I get from she?'

'You en show me nothing, child,' replied Miss De Young, putting on an aggrieved tone.

Mrs Steward hurried back to her desk to get the envelope from her bag. Miss De Young took it and began to sift through the pack of coloured photographs, exclaiming 'Aiee' after looking at each.

The photographs showed Mrs Steward's sister, a smiling lady in a pink woolly sweater in a series of poses, each calculated to show off her different household appliances – on a plump sofa with a television in the background, on a satiny bed, pouring herself a drink from a refrigerator.

'They come out nice. She resemble you,' said Miss De Young, who had been passing the pictures to the typist.

Just then the senior typist came across to find out if they each had a roll of toilet paper. Her duties also included seeing that everyone in the section had a glass to drink water from the ice pitcher, and a small hand towel.

Then Hartley came striding in, his thin, intense face oblivious to the hostile glances thrown in his direction.

'Well, well, aren't we all in our element,' he remarked to no one in particular, and with a flick of his wrist, he brushed his desk with his newspaper and settled himself in his grey swing chair.

It was remarks like those that made the others in the section wild. Hartley had lived in England for a while and unfortunately for him his voice was more English than Guianese, full of subtle sarcasm and innuendoes which everyone saw as an air of superiority. And as if that wasn't enough, Hartley defined himself as a 'Marxist-Leninist in embryo'. He didn't wear a collar and tie like the other civil servants, but dressed in an open-neck shirt and sandals and carried around with him a small haversack full of books by Marx and Engels and magazines about the situation in Cuba. Everyone knew he was in the YSO, the Young Socialist Organisation, the youth arm of Mohabir's party.

Dinah, who sat in the corner on the other side of the room, glanced across at Hartley but he wasn't looking in her direction. She liked him. She admired his boldness and the way he referred to his seniors as bureaucrats and philistines and predicted that the government was going to kick them out; the way he had of walking out of the endless staff meetings called by the head of the division, saying, 'I'm tired of all this crap.'

And recently a new complicity was developing between them. Hartley had taken to lending her some of his magazines about the Cuban revolution; about how Fidel and Che had overcome the tyranny of Batista; their concern for the peasants; the campaign to make them literate. The seeds of socialism began to tickle her toes.

Remembering her across the room, Hartley suddenly spun around, then got up and came over to her desk. With an unexpectedly sweet smile, his eyes settled on her face. 'So,' his voice rose in mockery, 'the gracious Duke leaves the seething cauldron today.'

'You seen him?' Dinah asked smiling, knowing what his reaction would be.

Unmindful of the stares, Hartley leapt into the air, 'O yes, I saw him, the Duke the Duke!' he sang, 'I wouldn't have missed him for the world.'

'Why weren't you at work yesterday, naughty girl?' he went on. 'You know what your supervisor would have to say.'

Dinah had taken her first day off from work yesterday, the first time in her four months at the Ministry, which was a good record. Nearly everyone else took a day off when they felt they had worked for a sufficiently long stretch to deserve one, which could be anything from two weeks to two months.

Dinah was just about to tell him when the head of the division, a short, moving bulk of a man came in, crooked a fat finger at her and moved towards his room. Everyone drifted reluctantly to their seats.

'Stupid old geeser,' said Hartley as Dinah rose and moved towards Mr Adams' door. In spite of her cool face she always felt a bit nervous when he called her and, bracing herself, she knocked louder than she intended on his door.

'Come in,' he barked. Dinah entered and was confronted with the familiar sight of him filling his chair behind a desk so laden with files and papers that it always amazed her how he ever found the space to write anything.

Mr Adams was what the Guianese called a red man – rust brown complexion, small deep-set eyes, heavy cheeks and a character that thrived on excitability. Coming upon her with Hartley at her desk meant Dinah was in for an even greater gruelling that morning.

'Why weren't you at work yesterday, Miss?' he asked in a deliberately low voice, gathering impact for the coming storm.

'I wasn't well, Mr Adams,' she lied, 'I telephoned and left a message with Miss De Young.'

Mr Adams stared at her for a brief hard moment, and then his voice broke. 'Miss Walcott, Miss Walcott, you're playing with your job, Miss. I've spoken to you time and time again, Miss, about the latecoming and now about this. We can't go on like this, Miss. We can't go on like this. This Ministry is in a very peculiar position. I don't think you're aware of what's happening in this Ministry, Miss. You're playing with your job, Miss. Why are you playing with your job, Miss? You know how much people out there would gladly take your place, Miss. Only waiting to take your job . . .'

Dinah, who had been through this many times before, tried to look suitably impressed by his words, tried to look as if he was striking a deep fear in her heart because she knew from her short experience that this meant less time in the long run. But she had been through it once too often and, try as she might, her face looked only more and more bored and impatient as he went on.

'I don't think you're aware of what's happening in this Ministry, Miss . . .'

'But Mr Adams, I told you I was sick. I can't help it if I wasn't well.' In spite of herself her voice rose.

'Don't be insolent, Miss. Don't be insolent,' he shouted, his face taking on an ugly look. 'Do you realise that you're still on probation and that I have to recommend you for confirmation?' he asked threateningly. 'You're very rude, Miss, and I'm going to write this in your personal file immediately. I have a good mind to call the Minister about this,' he bluffed, watching her face closely to see her reaction.

He was just about to rest a damp hand on the phone when the phone itself rang shrilly. Dinah got up to leave quickly, an old trick that worked at times, but this time he barked at her to sit down.

She sat back and waited.

It was Harding on the line from upstairs, and Mr Adams' voice changed to cloying familiarity. The two were on very good terms. Dinah guessed that the Minister and his Permanent Secretary were not in the building. Harding informed him, with what must have been grim satisfaction, that Singh, the East Indian supervisor upstairs, had just been appointed to the post of Chief Accountant.

'What!' Mr Adams bellowed, excitedly, 'You making fun, Horace. You mean we gone so bad. Man, Horace you making fun.'

Horace assured him that he wasn't making fun and Mr Adams said in a wondering kind of voice, 'I wonder how Martin gun take this, buddy,' Martin was the African senior who everyone felt would have got the job.

The conversation went on and then Mr Adams, just

remembering something, said with unrestrained glee, 'You know they picketing in front of Parliament again . . .' At this point Dinah rose to slip through the door and this time he didn't worry to stop her.

In the middle of the morning the entire staff was given permission to stand in the street if they wanted to to wave the Duke goodbye. Dinah and Hartley, the only two in their section not to take up the invitation, stood at the front windows drinking ice-water and exchanging supercilious little smiles as they watched the others outside.

Mr Adams gave them a cold look as he jostled his way down the steps to join them in a self-conscious rush of allegiance.

'Look at the philistines,' said Hartley, 'I tell you, girl, one of these days I going to put them all in a book. I'm going to enjoy writing about them, especially that big blunderer.' His eyes followed Mr Adams' bounding figure. 'They all happy to let the imperialists keep controlling this country.'

'Maybe the government should have a guerrilla force to back them up in the jungle,' said Dinah half-jokingly as she crunched a piece of ice.

Hartley gave her one of his intense stares, 'How come I didn't think of that? You're bloody right, you know.'

Jumbie lef he pipe yah
No-ka-no-ka
Wha kinda gate dis?
Iron gate dis
Yuh mean ah kyant break it?
No-ka-no-ka
Yuh mean ah kyant break it?
No-ka-no-ka . . .

You chant. Your friends make a ring and you chant,
moving around to break the ring of hands. You play
hopscotch, drawing circles and squares of chalk. You
play cricket, pulling the big rubbish bin into a wicket.
Friends come from all around the yard. Jamie, Mrs
Ramsammy grandson, with his jet black hair like the
seal at the zoo. Stella, Jeanette sister, and Teddy, the
Portuguese boy with spectacles, living a little way
down the road.

Sometimes you get tired of games and you and
Anthony sit on the bridge, swinging your feet in the
brown water below, watching the boys sitting under
the sandbox tree on the opposite side of the road,
interfering with nearly everybody going by:

65

Honey Bee Bottle
B-Bottle
Honey Bee Bottle
B-Bottle . . .

   That's the shout as the old East Indian man,
collecting bottles in a ricebag, make his way down the
street.
Walka de nigger
Walka de nigger . . .

   That's the shout as soon as you catch a glimpse of
the thin brown man, always carrying a big brick in his
hand, a brick he never use, never throw at anybody
no matter how much they call him, 'Walka de
nigger'. All he'd do is reply, 'British you fool,'
holding his big brick as if it was some kind of
prayer.

8

A few days after the Duke had left the country Conrad came around to take Archie to a political meeting being held by Mohabir at the Bourda Green that evening. Archie, who would not have even considered going on his own since he expected trouble, was going only because of Conrad. With Conrad beside him with his .38 revolver stuck deep in his back pocket, Archie always felt immeasurably safer.

Anyone would feel safe beside Conrad, that was if he happened to be their friend, for Conrad, an ex-photographer in the Criminal Investigation Department of the Police Force, had come into contact with most of the criminals in the country, including the Georgetown choke-and-robbers who left him strictly alone. As well they might have done, since apart from his revolver and strange appearance, Conrad knew the art of self-defence very well, having only to stick out one of his long legs at a certain angle to send anyone sprawling if he wished.

An extremely tall man in his early fifties, eyes turned to regard Conrad wherever he went. He wore khaki shorts, knee-length beige socks and a monocle in his left eye. His long thin face ended in a bristly outcrop of beard which he dyed red when it suited him and he had the habit of running his fingers like a plough through his soft woolly hair every few minutes, so his hair stood on edge like a mad genius. Conrad was not unflattered by the effect of his personality on people and sometimes deliberately wore a red jersey so that people would think him a communist. He also kept white mice as pets, sometimes walking around with a few and allowing them to disappear down his shirt front, and reappear, peeping out his sleeves. This intrigued Gem who began to live on his lap and shoulders.

On the evening of the meeting, it was still early when he arrived at the Walcotts and he had metem with them, cassava, plantains and eddoes boiled in coconut milk and topped with fried fish and ochroes. Conrad licked his plate unashamedly when he was finished and then they retired to the drawing room for a little while. 'It's the budget causing all this confusion and talk of general strike,' said Clara. 'If you give me the chance I'll just fly back to my little Highdam.'

'To tell you the truth, I don't think it's such a bad budget,' said Conrad, 'but the newspapers really going to town about it, man. What the *Chronicle* call it? Budget of Tears,' he guffawed, running his fingers through his hair. 'It's the increase in rum and beer and cigarettes that really got some people worried. But that won't keep them from the rumshops. You wait and see.'

'But Conrad, milk, aerated drinks, milo, sweetsoap all gone up,' said Clara a bit reprovingly. She sat on the old-fashioned settee, her ankles tucked slightly under her, her face taking on a beautifully grave expression.

'If the British had given Mohabir better loans, he wouldn't have had to draw up this kind of budget. And don't forget, the businessmen trying to cut back on their own taxes. Some of them increasing left, right and centre. Youall wouldn't feel the pinch, man,' Conrad went on in a teasing tone, 'Archie here is a rich man.'

'Rich! Hah,' Archie gave a short friendly snort, settling

back in his Berbice chair with a gloomy expression, his hands folded behind his head. 'I don't know what's happening to this country, man,' he added, referring to the news in the morning paper that had said the Trade Union Council was considering calling a general strike.

'Look,' said Conrad, leaning forward to pat his knee in an almost paternal way, 'You're too much of a worrier and worrying won't help things. In any case, you can't change the course of events, old boy. Something will break. This country will pass through a crisis. But things will change,' he said, stressing heavily on each of the 'wills', then adding, 'for better or for worse.'

Archie wasn't comforted. But that was how most of their conversations went these days, with Archie expressing his fears and Conrad trying to reassure him in his usual unperturbed manner.

The two men were old friends. At times Clara wondered how they, so vastly different, had become such good friends. He had known Conrad since his days on the Essequibo Coast when Conrad was stationed there, taking grisly murder photographs with meticulous care. Conrad had happened to fix Archie's Velo-Solex bicycle for him one day when it broke down on the road, and after that their friendship developed. Now that the Walcotts were living in the city, Conrad, who had always lived there, was a regular visitor. Conrad himself lived with his mother, a gentle, white-haired, old lady whom he cared for with utter devotion. He never married.

Archie, who didn't pry too deeply into Conrad's affairs, nevertheless got the impression that he never voted as he didn't believe in investing any politician with the power to make decisions about his life. But Conrad was well attuned to what was happening, not only in Guiana, but all around the world, his house full of radios and electric wires connecting him to the outside world. He also had a secret fondness for political meetings which he would attend, standing with an odd smile about his lips.

'But what I can't understand,' Archie said, as he massaged the side of his temples, 'is why he's so set on bringing communism to this country. And the thing is the Indians don't seem to mind. They would keep on voting for him at every election. I don't see how he could ever be displaced.'

'Man, Arch,' said Conrad, leaning forward, 'winning elections and carrying a country to independence is two different things, buddy. You think the English people 'tupid? Let them play 'tupid nuh, and they going have the Americans in their backsides. Look, neither Britain nor America going stand back and see the Russians take over this country. After all, is in their own interest, and let's face it, they interested in they own interest. Cuba was a mistake, as far as America concerned, and they not going to make it happen again. Another Cuba in the Caribbean! Impossible man.'

Conrad, who usually spoke of Cuba in an admiring tone, leaned back, slapped his leg, and pulled what he often referred to as his 'Fidel Castro beard'.

Archie always had a sneaking suspicion that Conrad was not totally unsympathetic to Mohabir. At this point the loud-speaker van, which had been announcing the meeting throughout the day, passed again and Clara decided on the spur of the moment that she would come down to the meeting too, as Dinah had just got back from the Badminton Club she had joined recently.

'Clar, you think you should?' Archie asked. 'These meetings always have trouble.' Sometimes, though not often, Archie shortened her name by a syllable as a kind of endearment.

But Clara, who had never been to a political meeting in Georgetown, was suddenly all curious.

'This international politics is a hell of a thing, buddy. You know the CIA got they people right under Mohabir nose,' said Conrad, continuing the conversation as they walked along. 'I tell you, you don't know what going on in this

70

place. The CIA boys come in all shapes and sizes. I know one American over here right now claiming to be on a wildlife research project. Wildlife, my ass!'

'Conrad, you always seem to be in the know,' Clara smiled. As they crossed over Durban Street, the groups of people drifting towards the meeting were picking up. From all appearances, it looked as if it was going to be one of those big noisy Georgetown political meetings. Already one or two people were cursing loudly as they went by, and Archie held Clara's arm.

'I can't cope with these disorderly crowds,' he said, as they drew nearer. 'I'm surprised Mohabir holding a meeting at a time like this.'

Conrad patted his pocket with his .38 reassuringly. The streets surrounding the Bourda Market square were blocked off by the police when they got there, and people were already standing all around. Conrad, Clara and Archie edged their way along until they came to the North Road corner, which was less crowded and gave a good view of the platform, brightly lit with a string of electric bulbs running above.

No sooner had the meeting begun than a gang of youths on bicycles started circling around, shouting out loudly, and bending over to brush the road with the PIP symbol, the mop, which the PIP leader, in one of his moments of oratory, had said was 'destined to mop up the dregs of imperialism'.

The market vendors, who had stalls outside the market, had put away their bananas and papaws and mangoes for the night, though the coconut vendors were very much there with their piles of water coconuts and flickering bottle lamps. The policemen weaved easily between the stalls and crowd. Not so many East Indian faces were to be seen as they were expecting trouble.

The Minister of Labour, a short stoutish Chinese man, one of the few on the political scene, was the first to speak and though interrupted constantly by loud heckling and the gang of moppers, he managed to outline some of the government's achievements, especially in the field of labour. At times his voice came over muffled, at times gratingly loud. The amplifiers were not working too well, and people had clearly not come to hear him. Their repeated cries of 'Done with the long talk!' were accompanied once by a rotten orange, hurled at the edge of the platform.

The Minister of Labour seemed not to notice, though a few moments later he remarked: 'They always complaining about unemployment, but the only employment some of them fit for is throwing rotten oranges.'

A muted roar ran through the crowd, then a rippling anticipation for the next speaker – the Premier himself.

Dressed casually in open-neck shirt, the Premier, his face showing signs of strain, was silent for a few moments before the microphone. Then he began to speak, his voice coming through surprisingly strong and passionate, almost agitated: 'Fellow Guianese, comrades all. We are gathered here tonight at a time when this country, your country, faces its worst economic crisis since we took office. You yourselves know that our sugar and rice industries haven't recovered from the severe drought experienced last year, and a huge deficit is already anticipated in our next budget . . .'

'That is because you spending de money on de coolie up the Corentyne,' someone in the crowd shouted.

'Mismanagement!' someone else shouted.

'In the face of this economic climate the People's Labour Party has had no alternative but to come up with a budget that seriously attempts to put our country on a firmer economic footing . . .'

'Mismanagement!' the voice screamed again.

'Like some of them come to these meetings just to interrupt,' Clara said.

'They don't want to hear facts and ideology, man,' Conrad said. 'Ideology don't win elections in this country. Race is the thing.'

'Anyway, let me listen to the man,' Clara said.

'We, the people of Guiana, must be responsible for our own national development. We cannot depend on foreign aid because we're not getting any. Believe me, comrades, we are not getting any. The British government has refused to consider any financial increases for our development plan, and time and time again we have been frustrated in our efforts to secure aid from those countries willing to lend us. To show you what I mean, just last year, after talks, the Cuban government agreed to lend us equipment and materials to the tune of thirty million Guiana dollars and to provide us with a loan to establish a wood pulp project. But this generous offer hasn't seen the light of day. Why comrades? I'll tell you why, comrades. Because right now it is being deliberately put in cold storage by the Colonial Office. I suppose they have to consult the US government first before they can make a decision,' he added sarcastically.

'Comrades, the objective of the British government is clear. Having failed to defeat us by divide and rule tactics, having failed to defeat us by suspending our constitution and throwing us in jail, they're now applying the economic squeeze to get us out of power. And the American government, in its anti-Soviet campaign and anti-Cuba propaganda, will stop at nothing to help them . . .'

At this point there was a sudden shattering sound and two of the electric bulbs, hanging above the platform, were knocked out by a brick. Mohabir, who had ducked his head instinctively at the sound, straightened up, glanced down at the light pieces of glass at the end of the platform, and said, 'I hope the police officers are taking note of this.'

There was a brief pause in the meeting, and two black policemen moved towards the platform.

Mohabir went on speaking: 'As for the Trade Union Council and their talk of calling a general strike, I can only say that at a time like this, it will result in nothing but economic disaster for this country. They speak about freedom and democracy, comrades, but they are puppets of the

British and American governments. Their aim is to get us out of power by bringing the country to a standstill, and to halt our march to independence. They are only using the budget as a scapegoat . . .'

A voice in the crowd, at the mention of the word scapegoat, broke into a loud series of goatlike 'mmmaaayys'.

Above the laughter, Mohabir continued: 'But I say this, comrades, they will not stop the tide of history . . .'

At this point, there was another shattering. A few more electric lights went, and sensing more trouble, Archie, Clara and Conrad began drifting away.

'My people, my people,' Archie said, shaking his head.

'These Georgetown meetings,' said Clara as Mohabir's agitated voice followed them.

There is nobody else like him. Who else could make white mice disappear down their shirt collar and reappear, peeping out at the cuff of their sleeve?

Who could boil milo, your favourite treat, like him? Putting a whole unopened tin of milo in a pot of boiling water. Letting it boil and boil and boil till all the chocolately brown grains come together in a hard glossy cake of milo toffee.

He said you were a clever child. You were going to be somebody great when you grew up. You're wiser than your ten years.

Sitting across his shoulders, hands locked under his chin, skirt bunched around your thighs, brown legs wrapped around his sides, he is like a new father.

Sitting on his lap, arms draped around his neck, you tell him all your jokes. 'Conrad,' you say, 'you hear the latest news?'

'No, what's the latest news?'

'An ant got knocked down by a bus on Camp Street this afternoon,' you say and can't stop laughing at the idea.

And because you love him, you let him nibble your

ears and press you against him, smelling his special scent of liquorice and photographs.

You love going to his small photo studio which is near the Public Library. Every afternoon you go to the Library then visit Conrad afterwards, rushing home from school and rushing back out again.

Conrad is always pottering around at the back of his studio. You like standing before the sinks of floating photographs, watching the pale outlines becoming darker and darker, as Conrad keep switching them from one sink to another. Sometimes you even help him to put them on that shiny metal sheet to dry.

9

'Are you going on the march, Miss?' Mr Adams enquired of Dinah in an innocent enough voice.

'I suppose so,' Dinah smiled back evasively. At times, though she didn't know why, Dinah felt a bit sorry for 'the blunderer', caught as he was between his natural affinity for the British and the semblance of loyalty he had to show towards his 'communist' government employers – an intolerable colonialist situation that was putting a big strain on him, making him more careful about what he said on the phone to Harding upstairs, stretching the impartiality he tried to show to breaking point.

'We civil servants must be loyal to the government of the day. Must be impartial,' he'd take care to say, glancing around him whenever he had one of his staff meetings.

Now he was smiling at Dinah mysteriously: 'Of course it's your business what you do and who you mix with, but this Ministry is in a very peculiar position. A very peculiar position. Don't say I didn't warn you, Miss.'

Why couldn't he just say outright that she ought to go on the march instead of all the beating around the bush? Dinah stared at him.

'Nobody is forcing you to go, Miss, but if you don't go

you'll have to remain at the Ministry and work,' he concluded bluntly, dismissing her.

But Dinah was feeling in a dangerous mood. She didn't want to march since she wasn't against the budget, or for that matter the government. The thought of being one of the few at work in her department didn't appeal to her either.

'Maybe we can just show our faces at the Union Hall and then shoot off,' she said to Hartley in a tone of conspiracy. 'Check out the scene around Georgetown. Maybe end up at the Parade Ground to hear the outcome of the march later in the afternoon.'

'Naughty, naughty,' grinned Hartley. 'We are corruptible, aren't we?'

While the rest of the Ministry staff were leaving in batches and drifting down Brickdam to commence the march, Hartley rolled Dinah's bicycle out of the sprawling sandy yard. The drivers regarded them with an indolent inquisitiveness and though she prided herself on not giving a damn what people thought, Dinah suddenly felt very conscious of the intimate picture she and Hartley must be cutting.

Just before hopping on to the carrier behind, she experienced a paralysing fear that they would fall. She could almost hear the sound of the men's raucous laughter behind her. But though the bicycle wobbled a little, Hartley braced his thin sinewy arms and they rode out into the street.

They spent no time at all at the Civil Service Union, which was teeming with the more middle class of Guianese society, servants from all the different Ministries, batches already out in the streets with pickets and banners.

Dinah and Hartley boldly made their way around to the quieter side street, and were soon riding again, checking out the Georgetown scene, rounding the slight curve by the Botanical Gardens, the sun beating down on their heads, trade winds blowing against Hartley's chest. Swinging towards Dinah, he said, 'Well, as the tourist brochure would say, here's your "Garden City of the Caribbean".'

Dinah grinned, 'Don't forget our labba and creekwater. You ever eat labba?'

'Once when I was in the interior on a scout trip. That was before I left for Britannia. I suppose that's why I'm back. You know the old saying? Eat labba, drink creekwater, you must return to Guiana. Talking about creekwater,' went on Hartley, 'I'm kind of thirsty. I don't know about you. Feel like a drink?'

At the Tower View Hotel a few whites were sitting out at tables under huge cloth umbrellas, skins ranging from the seasoned rusty brown to the bright and peeling pink of the newly arrived. The bar at the front of the hotel was open to locals but few Guianese ever came here, the atmosphere and prices exceeding all expectations.

He and Dinah sat at one of the shady tables on the outskirts of the bar, while the brown and black waiters weaved suavely in and about. After about ten minutes, Hartley said in an imperious voice, 'Can we get some service this side, please?'

A couple of white heads turned for a quick stare and a moment later an Indian waiter came across to take their order with the condescending tolerance he reserved for 'locals'.

Dinah scrutinised the menu with over-deliberate thoroughness, knowing full well they intended ordering only two glasses of orange juice.

'Two glasses of orange juice, please,' Hartley ordered, tipping his chair backwards and Dinah stressed, 'with plenty ice.'

'These people,' Hartley said, nodding in the direction of the whites, 'you've ever been to any of the sugar estates and see how they live with their exclusive clubs, swimming pools and what have you? Girl, I tell you these expatriates have built their empires on sugar and tea.'

'Only the other day, a cousin of mine was talking about Hope Estate and the rundown logie-shacks,' added Dinah. 'He say how the sugar workers live in real squalor.'

'The government should nationalise the blasted sugar industry,' said Hartley, not realising how much he'd raised his voice.

'Not so loud,' said Dinah, as a few more heads turned in their direction.

'But the government don't have any real power, you know,' Hartley continued in a quieter tone, spinning his glass around, 'the Mother Country still decides on just about every important issue.'

'What I can't understand,' said Dinah passionately, 'is why Guianese people can't pull together, to work for the good of the country. Everybody pulling everybody down. Everything is race. If anyone get promotion in the Ministry, is because of race. The East Indians for Mohabir because he's East Indian. The black people for Atwell because he black. The Portuguese and coloured people for Ferreira, because he's Portuguese. People don't seem to be looking at what the party stands for.'

Hartley looked at her with a new glint in his eyes. 'Well, they've done a good job of divide and rule, the British,' he said. 'Keep the natives occupied with strife. Keep them suspicious of one another while we walk off with the cake. It's the old colonial story. You only have to look at our history to see how the whole labour force was divided up. When the African workers, after slavery, wanted more for their labour, the planters had a cheap supply of workers from India to turn to. Don't forget the British were in India at the time. Then they talked about "unreliable African labour" and "reliable Indian labour" while exploiting the East Indians and setting them in competition against the Africans.'

Dinah crossed her legs, feeling both sophisticated and daring. Sophisticated because here she was at this expensive outdoor bar, sitting in the shade of small palm trees and hibiscus hedges, discussing politics. Daring because of her evasion of both march and work.

'But the East Indians themselves always talk about working on the plantation as a kind of slavery,' she said, 'is hard work, my cousin, the one I was just talking about, he made me laugh. He said he worked a day as a canecutter. He left early in the morning with his little saucepan of food. A truck picked him up, along with the other canecutters. At the end of the day he said his own mother couldn't recognise him. He went home deadbeat, his face like leather from all the sun and smoke. You know they burn the cane leaves before cutting the cane? He said that was the first and last day he worked as canecutter. Now everybody does call him "Baboolall".' Dinah giggled at the memory of her cousin.

'Indian sugar workers, black bauxite workers, rice farmers, they all have to come together in a united front,' said Hartley. 'As Marx maintained, you can't fight the capitalists with a divided labour force. People haven't given Mohabir a chance. All this bloody fuss about the budget and demonstrations. The budget is just being used as a scapegoat by the trade unions.'

From the corner of her eye Dinah detected the waiters hovering in their white jackets. She and Hartley had long finished their drinks, and since the price indeed exceeded their expectation, they didn't have another.

When Dinah and Hartley finally reached the Parade Ground, the scene of the mass demonstration, the sun was cooler and the tired sweaty marchers were listening to the address by the Trade Union president himself.

And it was dusk when the news of the general strike carried through the streets of Georgetown like windblown bits of burnt cane leaves.

Conrad got a picture of you on his wall. He took it with you sitting on a low stool. You remember the bright lights on your face. The black hood over his face and then the lights coming before you could fix your mouth in a proper smile.

You like going into the dark room with him and seeing the last bit of light, blotting out with the closing of the door. It's always pitch black inside the dark room and so quiet you could almost hear his breathing. Your eyes strain against the darkness, trying to find a speck of light to tell you that you're not blind. You're quite alone in time and darkness with Conrad, until he put on that light on his developing machine. Sometimes you're glad when he opens the door again though.

10

Archie had got into the habit of spending most of his mornings out. He had to have something to do. Usually his morning routine consisted of searching the Stabroek Market wharf for fruit bargains, slightly touched hands of bananas and mangoes. Exchanging a book at the library, if he had to do that, and sitting around to read some of the foreign newspapers. Visiting a hardware shop to pick up some bit of household tool. Sometimes buying the meat for Clara's cooking the following day. In the evenings he gave private lessons to the children of some of his old friends to bring in some extra money.

The cost of living in Georgetown was much higher than in Highdam where free fresh fish and vegetables had come by so easily. Since moving, Archie felt he had spent a fortune. It seemed that the children were always making some new demand on him. If it wasn't money for books, it was for PE clothes or some outing. He felt the teachers were carrying on a racket, making parents buy a lot of expensive books they hardly ever used. He bought only the children's exercise books and one or two text books and told them to ask their teachers if they felt he had a money tree.

Clara spent a big part of the morning cooking. Though

she hated the headache of having to think up what to cook every day, she enjoyed the act of cooking and was totally consumed in it, surrounded by bowls and brown paper bags and spices and vegetable skins. Her favourite dish, one she cooked with increasing regularity, was fufu, green plantains boiled and pounded into a smooth, slightly sticky firmness, accompanied by a luscious beef curry. While the pieces of meat soaked up the lemon juice and garlic and curry paste and eschalot and wiri-wiri peppers, Clara would pound the fufu in her sturdy wooden mortar. She kept up the rhythm with the long, smooth, thick pestle, up and down, round and round, getting the bits from the sides of the mortar and working them in, dipping the pestle into a nearby bowl of water. Moist and magical, embodying at once all the diverse ingredients of her culture in this act of pounding fufu, Clara would pause to sip from a cup of imported English Red Rose tea.

But after cooking and eating she didn't want to see the kitchen. She thought it was an insult to the stomach to think of clearing and washing up after enjoying good food and she had to keep reminding Archie of one of her old cousin's sayings: 'housework never done and I for one didn't come down to this earth to finish it'.

So the afternoons, after the children had left for school and Dinah for work, saw Clara taking a shower to cool herself down, lightly sprinkling Mennens baby powder between the cleft of her young-looking breasts, sapping her head with Limacol (the freshness of a breeze in a bottle as the manufacturers called it), throwing herself into bed and covering her eyes from the glare of the light with a piece of cloth. A woman needed time alone to regain her equilibrium.

These days Clara's thoughts kept drifting towards the musical career she thought she had sacrificed for marriage and children, and kept seeing a vision of herself in blue silk, hair swept up in a roll playing the piano to a large appreciative audience.

Sometimes, when she didn't have the cloth covering her

eyes from the light, she'd let her gaze follow the darting movement of a small house lizard across the bedroom ceiling, a smile coming to her lips whenever she remembered the story of the white lady who was driven back to living in England because she couldn't stand the sight of 'those little crocodiles in the ceiling'.

Clara missed Rose and the other Highdam people, but especially Rose – the belly laughs, the one-to-one fullness whenever she and Rose were together. Not having Rose come over to see her nearly every day, or she going across to see Rose was like having a piece of herself damped out.

At these times Clara's thoughts would inevitably extend to her parents, both dead, dwelling on the good memories of her childhood. Recalling her mother shelling hot parched nuts for them on the front steps on a Friday night. Recalling with a half-smile the time when her father gave her – Clara was seven then – her first and only little slap for unscrewing the kitchen tap and flooding the entire kitchen floor. Just a year after her marriage to Archie, Clara's father had died.

Archie often joined her in bed amid these thoughts, and contrary to what their children supposed, they did do it when the mood was right.

At times Clara felt more saddened than angry over Archie's meanness and tried to find excuses for him. It wasn't so much that he was mean, but rather he was crippled with the fear of losing all he had. It was this fear of poverty that he was ever guarding against which made him mean. At other times she wasn't so understanding though. Like with the fridge.

The fridge. Ever since moving to Georgetown Clara had been singing the merits of a refrigerator. Apart from satisfying her own craving for ice cold water which she had developed since coming to the city (the Georgetown water was dull and flat, not refreshing like Highdam), she said that with a fridge they wouldn't have to buy so piecey-

piecey every day and that they could even make custard blocks to sell so that the fridge would pay for itself.

'The school children from Gem and Anthony's school would only be too glad to come and buy,' she assured Archie, 'you know how school children like their custard blocks and fluties.'

Archie appeared to have been persuaded, nearly every household seemed to have a fridge these days, and even had a wooden stand built for it. But in a last-minute panic of how much it was going to deplete his account, he changed his mind.

To spite him, Clara had started to run up a credit account at the small Chinese supermarket, though in all fairness, she did feel that they needed the extra food. She now owed the Chinese man about thirty dollars and had no idea how she was going to pay it. When the crunch came, Archie would have to fork it out, she supposed. But she knew he wouldn't take it lightly. In fact, she had a very good idea how he would take it. She just refused to think about it, experiencing a nervous excitement whenever she did.

Archie found out about it sooner than she meant him to because they had a terrible row on the evening that the general strike was announced.

Clara was convinced that they hadn't enough food in the house to see them through, however long the strike was going to last. Archie appeared indifferent.

'What you want me to do?' he asked from his reclining position in the Berbice chair. 'Rush out and start buying like a madman?'

'If your own mother self was dying you wouldn't rush out and start buying like a madman,' said Clara hotly, 'I don't expect you to buy like a madman. I only expect you to show some concern for the well-being of your children.'

And the row had taken off from there, the two of them following each other around the house, hunting each other down with goading remarks. Archie referring to 'the state' in which she kept the house, which had no bearing on the present crisis. Clara, trembling, blood up in her head, controlling the urge to pick up a knife by picking up other things. Revealing her account at the Chinese shop.

Archie, a greyish pallor coming to his dark face at the news, a muscle jumping under his left cheekbone. 'If you're going to be a spendthrift, then you'll have to stand the consequences.'

'If you think me and my children are going to stay here and starve, you're making a sad mistake,' declared Clara.

'Your trouble is that you have life too easy,' provoked Archie.

'Easy, hell,' raved Clara, who was in fact very industrious, always dyeing the children's school uniforms so that they would look bright and fresh, darning and patching Archie's clothes, putting tasty dishes together from all kinds of bits and pieces, and never having any money of her own.

'A lady of leisure,' said Archie.

'Even your own friends have to talk about you,' said Clara. 'That man wouldn't give away a sugarcake if he could help it.'

Clara was driven into bringing up the 'sugarcake story' though she herself didn't laugh when Wilma told her that Martin, an old family friend from their Essequibo days, had said that about Archie – him not giving away a sugarcake if he could help it. It was one thing to criticise your husband to your friends. Quite another when they did the criticising and ridiculing. And in a way it reflected upon her as she had done the choosing of Archie.

Clara's remark about what Martin had said achieved the required effect on Archie and he began to drum his fingers irritatingly on the window sill.

'If you think me and my children going starve,' repeated Clara.

Archie did go out in the end, returning with a case of evaporated milk, some rations of rice and sugar and in the morning she found some more money for her, resting on the vanity. But they weren't on talking terms.

The atmosphere at the breakfast table was strained. There were light shadows under her eyes and he sat eating his egg, tight-lipped.

Gem, watching her father slowly chewing his food – Archie was always stressing the importance of chewing food – suddenly burst out laughing at the table, sending little bits of wet bread flying. Anthony too began to grin, ducking his head under the table to avoid his father's eyes.

'Life is happy, eh?' said Archie. 'Nothing to do but laugh, eat and play. When you're hungry food appears on the table like magic. You have no idea how it gets here and no interest either.'

Gem went on laughing, making stifled little sounds to stop herself. At another time Clara might have joined in, her shoulders shaking.

'I bet you I give you something to laugh about,' cried Archie suddenly, rising up from the table and rushing across to his cupboard to get the wild cane. But Gem was too quick for him, running to the toilet and locking herself in.

Today they were all home because of the strike. Dinah, who ate when it suited her, was in the bedroom pressing her hair with a hot comb in front of the mirror, a towel across her neck. Clara was always telling her that she wouldn't be satisfied until all her hair had dropped out. Clara herself wore her lightly crinkled hair pinned back, and only gave it a touching up with the hot comb when she had some very special occasion.

Archie might still have gone out that morning if it wasn't for the Premier's speech. Mohabir came on the air about 10 a.m. He said that it had come to his knowledge that violence was being planned by certain elements, aimed at overthrowing the legally elected government. He said that the budget was only being used as a scapegoat for the

88

general plan which had the backing of CIA agents in the country. He blamed the Trade Union Council for calling a general strike, saying that he had in fact set a date to reconsider the budget. He also said that it had come to his knowledge that attempts against his own life would be made and warned all Guianese to stay in their homes.

The speech threw an immediate veil of apprehension over the household and Clara, who championed the under-dog in any situation, suddenly found herself being moved by Mohabir. Archie gave a grim 'Huh', feeling that the man had only himself to blame for getting the whole country into this state.

Lurleena, the new girl who come to live in the house
at the side of the passageway opposite Mr Castello.
Lurleena, tall, thin, dark with short neat plaits
around her head. Lurleena with her wide smile and
slightly crooked teeth. Lurleena with her bad temper.
The two of you become inseparable. You live at her
house. She at yours. 'The two of you like batty and
poe,' her grandmother would say. 'The two of you too
bewitched,' your mother would say. You like the same
kinds of books; schoolgirl and superman comics, Enid
Blyton, Nancy Drew mysteries. You play concerts on
her bed, using the bedstead as stage, dancing on the
springs, driving her grandmother wild. Then the two
of you would get to the window, throwing tiny bricks
on Mr Castello rooftop, ducking and giggling when he
come out and start to curse. Sometimes you play ole
higue. You like being the ole higue, glad for the
chance to come hobbling along in an old sheet, then
quietly pulling back the covers off Lurleena and
nibbling at her neck. She would start shrieking and
laughing the moment you reach the bed.
  Sometimes you play husband and wife, spreading

ricebags under the steps, shutting off the sides with pieces of boards and boxes so no one could see. Lying quietly together in a tangle of legs.

11

Ivy Payne groaned, turned, lifted herself up, her elbows supporting her body on the hard fibre mattress that lay on a bed of wooden planks. She stayed that way for a few nodding moments, then gently hoisted herself over the sleeping limbs of her children and stumbled, not quite fully awake, into the dark passageway that led to the kitchen. On her way she passed a small bedroom in which her eldest son and his wife and child were sleeping. Her second son, Vibert, had again slept out for she couldn't see his long, awkward frame curled up on the bedding on the drawing room floor.

Ivy didn't feel like going down to the yard bathroom and contented herself with splashing cold water on her face at the back window, scrubbing her teeth with some kitchen salt and rinsing the night away.

Today was Friday and she must hurry down to the abattoir before all the good runners and blood for her black pudding were sold out. She had taken up with the business ever since her trawler fishing husband had died four years ago, leaving her with the six children. After his death she was forced to sell their Broad Street cakeshop and take up residence in one of the Ramsammys' rundown little houses in the Charlestown yard. She supported herself and children with the black pudding money and from what she made at her weekly Saturday night dances. She couldn't depend on her eldest son for anything, now that he had his own family. But she did get some extra help from her manfriend, Cyril.

Cyril, a plumpish middle-aged man, came about twice a week. On these occasions Ivy made up a bed for the other children on the floor outside with Vibert so they would have some privacy. Cyril always came very late at nights, picking his way around the sleeping bodies and left in the morning before they woke up. He himself worked on the waterfront as a stevedore and his contributions to Ivy's family came in useful.

Vibert hated the best bone in Cyril for reasons peculiar to himself. At nineteen he was sullen and brooding and at nights would lie staring at the quiet face of his father's photograph which his mother had carefully hung on the drawing room wall. He could hear the shaking of the bed in his brother's room. He could endure that. What he couldn't stand was the sight of his mother's locked door and the knowledge that Cyril was inside there with her.

The thought of Cyril's smooth body and slick hair next to his mother's healthy darkness aroused such a fury in him. He felt she had no shame. He remembered the way she had carried on at his father's funeral, throwing herself across the coffin, but that was like a woman all over, he thought, quick to forget. Now he had to restrain himself from kicking the shaky door in and dragging the man out of the house, down the steps and right through the passageway. Also the way his mother had of putting aside Cyril's food first in the glass bowl made him sour inside.

Ever since the night that Vibert had ripped away her nightdress Ivy felt that some indefinable thread in the relationship between mother and son had been severed. That was the last time she had tried beating him.

Vibert would always remember the look of outraged

astonishment on her face, her tears afterwards. He didn't know what had possessed him that night. It had nothing to do with her shouting that he had no ambition or the blows she rained about his head and neck. In the act of deliberately ripping her nightdress he thought he was showing her the complete disrespect which he felt he now had for her.

Ivy lit the kerosene stove in the kitchen, then hurried back to the bedroom to dress. When she came out she added three heaping potspoons of sugar to the water on the stove, unplugged two tiny balls of paper from a tin of evaporated milk and poured a little in. She didn't trust her biggest girl, June, with the milk. She lifted down a basket of bread which she had baked the day before and placed a tin of margarine beside it. June would give the others their bread and tea later. Ivy helped herself only to a cup of the hot thin tea as she didn't want to get wind in her stomach, then she tied her head with a blue headtie, picked up her red shopping bag and hurried out of the house.

She picked her way along the passageway, stepping on the odd pieces of board precariously laid down. Apart from the clanking of pans which came from Mrs Lall's hut and which only reinforced Ivy's belief that she was haunted, the yard was still asleep. Ivy passed the remaining range rooms, patches of black crouching in the softening dawn, and stepped out into the cool streets.

She walked like a woman filled with sweet life, the red shopping bag with two large brown bottles fitted snugly into the crook of her arm, her cotton shift of red and yellow flowers blowing gently at the knees of her sturdy polished legs. A pale half moon still hovered in the skies and the streets had hardly begun to stir. Passing a rumshop, Ivy spat at the scent of urine that would dissipate itself in the sunshine later in the day.

She liked to start a day like this, untouched by the hungry, peevish faces of her children or the bawling of her son's baby. On days like this she felt strong, basking in her ability to cut and contrive and to make a living for her

94

children. It wasn't good to depend on any man and, even though she appreciated Cyril's help, she intended to make life her own way.

Ivy's thoughts continued to flow in serene contentment until she neared the Stabroek Market with all the buses lined up from the night before. Then it all came back. The news about the general strike last night.

Ivy stopped in her tracks, the red bag slipped down her arm to her fingers. 'Oh Christ! I forget everything bout dis kiss-me-ass-strike,' the words broke involuntarily from her lips in a strangled kind of way. 'Shit,' she went on, sucking her teeth, 'don't tell me dis going mean I kyant get no runners and blood to buy.' Ivy looked around in agitation as if seeking someone to tell her just what the strike would mean.

When she had heard the news from her eldest son, Marcus, last night, the thought that it would affect her black pudding had never entered her head for some reason. Now realisation was beginning to dawn.

Ivy stood there in a fit of indecision for a full five minutes. Across by the market she could see a few vendors standing uncertainly around their boxes of produce. Then she decided that she wouldn't turn back. She would go down to the abattoir and beg someone there to help her. There must be someone there, one of the men she joked with week after week. She didn't mind waiting the entire morning just as long as she got some blood and runners. She had come to depend too much on it, not only the money which made things stretch far into the week, but on the activity itself, the stuffing and the boiling and the cutting in a kitchen full of the scents of thyme and peppers, while every few minutes someone came around to the back door for a 'fifty cents black pudding' or 'a dollar black pudding.'

Ivy was just in time to see the night watchman rolling his bicycle away from the faded government abattoir building as she swung the corner into the street. He was moving away from her and she raised her arms and began to clap frantically, calling, 'Hee-ooo, hee-ooo.'

He heard her and turned his bicycle around. 'Is what you doing here, girl? You en hear bout de strike?' he asked as he came near her.

'Jesus Christ,' said Ivy.

'Is where you living girl?' he chided her.

'But I must get mih blood and runners,' said Ivy. 'You kyant help me?'

'Me!' he exclaimed, 'Sista, I would advise you to go home. You wasting yuh time waiting here. Nobody coming to work here dis morning. You see me. Is home I going home. No more nightshift till I hear dis strike call off. I would advise you to go home. When dem abattoir people come down here they en coming to work. They coming fuh demonstrate like de union say. I been at the meeting yesterday an I know what I talking bout.'

Ivy was only half listening to him. Already she could visualise how hard the coming week would be if she failed. But when the watchman suggested slyly that she meet him later that afternoon, her eyes returned swiftly to the present, and with a 'haul yuh ole tail', she sent him riding slowly away.

Ivy could feel the fingers of the sun eating into the hollow of her back, could feel the cool little trickles of perspiration running down her neck. She had been waiting for hours outside the abattoir along with four other women, all regular black puddings makers, all sticking around to see if they would have any luck. So far no luck.

The workers inside the compound who kept arriving in ones and twos were there to picket, not work. Some squatted in front of the main doorway in the shade while the bolder ones walked slowly up and down to display the placards pinned on their chests. Fresh from yesterday's bidding by the union, they were determined to play their part.

Ivy went up to one of the women carrying placards to find out exactly what was going on. The woman whose sign

96

read, 'Workers Will Die For Their Rights', simply said, 'Is up to youall if you want to wait but I don't think the abattoir opening up today.'

The other black pudding women didn't seem as put out as Ivy. In fact they seemed to be enjoying the novelty of seeing women like themselves strolling up and down with placards.

'Come, Ivy girl, what you going do?' they advised her with good-humoured resignation. 'Don't let lil black pudding money kill yuh.'

'We have to do something to bring down this bold face cammanist,' Mavis, a hardened women, philosophised.

Ivy sucked her teeth. 'What de hell you know bout cammanist?' she said contemptuously.

'But how yuh mean, mih dear darling,' retorted Mavis, 'dem cammanists does take away everything. Down to yuh own quarter pound here,' she said, putting her hand protectively between her legs, 'yuh can't call yuh own.'

A burst of belly laughter followed.

'Mind yuh jokes, Mavis, yuh know I have a weak bladder,' another woman admonished.

After a while Ivy detached herself from the women and went up to the man leaning against the door. She had seen him several times before giving orders inside the abattoir.

'God, this woman ent mean to give up,' said the man. 'Look lady, you don't understand a strike on? The store close. Nobody working today, an I can't help you. You going just have to do without de lil black pudding money this week.'

Midday, and the sun glinting harshly on galvanised zinc roofs; glistening on the heavy brown of the Demerara River; wilting the heads of hibiscus flowers; beating down on the mass demonstration at the parade ground, and on the different pickets being staged in front of government buildings around Georgetown.

The police, responding to the government's ban on all

public meetings, were on their way, not so much out of concern or sympathy with the government, but just complying with orders from their chief. Truckoads of them with batons and shields and teargas began to arrive at the various scenes.

Outside the Ministry of Labour, a crowd had already entrenched itself. Women were sitting flat out in front of the building, thighs spread out before them like giant hams. As the black-clad figures hopped out of the police truck, the women broke into the workers' song; 'We shall not, no, we shall not be moved. We shall not, no, we shall not be moved. Just like the trees standing by the water, we shall not be moved.'

The women indeed looked as if they couldn't be moved, massive flesh sunk below, making themselves as heavy as possible. The police regarded them hesitantly. Each face wore the same taunting provocative expression, daring to be moved.

But the police had to do something. Two young policemen each placed a hand under the sweating armpits of a woman and heaved. A tall woman got up and deliberately threw herself against one of the policemen, twisting the angle of his hat, and turning to the crowd; 'Yuh see. Yuh see. Yuh see how he push me?'

'Yes, we see. We see. We see how he push yuh,' the crowd chanted back.

At the electricity company the mood was ugly as crowds sent bricks and bottles flying into the building in protest at the work still taking place inside by some staff members.

'All you scabs, bring yuh tail out here,' was the cry. As the bricks and bottles increased the police moved in. People rushed madly to escape the sudden fumes of teargas, stumbling into nearby yards for water to wet their faces. A woman cried out, 'O God, de gas choking me baby.'

Even though the baby recovered, rumour spread that police teargas had just killed a baby. Two babies.

And that was all it took to set gangs of youths who had

attached themselves to the pickets and demonstrations kicking over street bins and smashing store windows.

Ivy and Mavis were still on the streets when news reached them that looting had started and the white superintendent of police had just been shot in another part of the city.

'Something been telling me all marning dat dis woulda happen,' said Mavis, panting to keep up with Ivy.

From the smaller side streets they could see people swarming out to join the crowds. Ivy even recognised some of the prostitutes who strolled around the Tiger Bay area.

'Wha happen? Wha happen?' she said, running forward a little to stop the man panting heavily towards them on his bicycle. But the man, his dark face oozing perspiration, didn't stop. 'Is madness break loose,' he said, continuing on his way.

Another man flew by, doubled over his bicycle handles, laden down with all sorts of bags, three shoe boxes clipped on to the carrier at the back of his bike, two new umbrellas still in their plastic cases dangling from the back of his collar.

'Christ!' said Ivy, standing still for a moment and watching the thickening movement of people ahead of her.

As she and Mavis got closer to the crowds and stores, they could see that the looting was in full swing. Men, women and youngsters, looking as if they'd just been through a bad scuffle, emerged from stores with bolts of cloth, shoes, arms full of clothing, anything they could manage to carry. Seeing one rumpled woman stagger past her with arms full of bath towels and nylon panties, Ivy was suddenly filled with the same madness. Good underwear is a luxury.

With Mavis' bony fingers clutching her arm, she half ran to the other side of the road and pressed herself against the mob of people now trying to get into another store, Singh & Sons Ltd. Pushed from behind, her own body was squashed up against the hardness of a man's wet back, the scent of his sweat filling her nostrils.

The next moment she was swept into the store, minus Mavis on her arm. The only thought in Ivy's head was to grab as much as possible. Things like this didn't happen every day. With a fearful exhilaration she was thrust again, this time with more than a dozen other people, into an aisle packed with brand new clothing and a counter with bolt upon bolt of cloth.

Ivy decided to forget the bolts of cloth. They would only hinder her, she needed her hands. But she must hurry, more and more people coming in, snatching left right and centre.

A man chucked her out of the way; 'When you getting freeness, lady, you can't pick and choose.'

Possessed, Ivy began to grab. About a dozen negligees from an open box on the top shelf; another open box of men's shirts; a handful of half-slips from below; some brassieres. Shirts under her arm and other things stuffed into her red bag, Ivy looked further down the line to a bottom shelf of lacy panties disappearing with lightning swiftness, some into a man's shirt front, some into a woman's bosom. By the time Ivy got to the shelf only crumpled plastic wrapping remained.

The store was hot and crowded now with people snatching just about anything, even two left-side shoes. At the back a raging tug-o-war was going on for bolts of cloth.

Ivy, who was almost being suffocated, pushed her way through on to the pavement, her neatly brushed, back-pressed hair standing in tufts all over her head.

You wonder about her, Miss Sheila. Did she really throw that acid on Mr Percy face? Because she look so quiet. If she did, did he really forgive her or only pretending? Why she didn't go out like the other women to the shops and stores and market? Why only looking through her window, dressed up, with that smile on her face? One day she ask you to buy a pack of biscuits from the shop for her. You run up her clean wooden steps quickly, but you can't really see inside her house properly. She hand you the money at the door and when you come back let you keep the three cents change.

But one day you discover you can see into her house, at least into her drawing room, from a small round hole in your toilet. Sometimes you peep at her and she don't even know. Sometimes she'd walk around in a pink half-slip alone and you see her nice big heavy breasts, just a shade lighter than the rest of her skin. You stare, wondering about she and Mr Percy, touching your own tiny breasts, only a little bigger than the halves of a twin guenip.

12

It was Gem who heard the urgency in the voice of the old Indian woman next door.

'Nabe, Nabe!'

Perhaps it was the urgency in the voice that made her drop her book so quickly and rush to the back window.

'You want something, Mrs Lall?' Gem inquired breathlessly, sensing instinctively that something was wrong.

'Tell yuh mudda to look quick,' Mrs Lall managed, leaning heavily against the wooden paling, a strange ashy look about her face.

'Mummy, Mrs Lall say to look quick,' Gem called out, startled by the fright she saw in the old woman's face.

Clara came in swiftly, wiping her soapy hands on the end of her dress, her brow knitting into its familiar pucker whenever she suspected something was wrong.

'Mrs Lall,' she pushed her head out of the window in a half-confiding, half-alarmed manner.

'Nabe, nabe, the town pan fire,' the words came out in a plaintive cry.

Clara's face paled. 'Fire, which fire?' she asked in bewilderment.

'Owh nabe, dem ah burn down de whole town. Dem

thiefing up everything in de stores and market dem. Ah prapa run, nabe. Look to de front window, de fire all bout de sky.'

At this point Gem listened no further. She ran to the front window and was confronted by the unmistakable smoke and flames blotting the northern skies. Her cry sent her father, who was resting inside, leaping up, and Dinah and Anthony too. Behind them Clara was witnessing the scene, three distinctive fires, in quiet amazement.

'God, to think all this going on and we don't know a word,' her voice held a note of accusation. Archie had turned the radio off earlier in the day, a natural act of conservation on his part.

The news of the fire and looting seemed to have reached the rest of the Charlestown yard at the same time, for moments later, snatches of excited conversation could be heard all around the yard.

Dinah and Clara went back to the kitchen window to listen to the rest of Mrs Lall's distraught outpourings. The Ramsammys closed up their rumshop quickly and Mrs Ramsammy hurried down from the big house to join Mrs Lall at the paling, walking in quick, agitated steps.

The two children, Gem and Anthony, bounded around the house. The sight of the flames seemed to have released a mad surge within them as they grappled with the two emotions, excitement and fear.

'Control yourselves,' snapped Archie as they collided with him in the passageway. But a grimness had settled over his own countenance. When he switched back on the radio only a solemn interlude of music was coming through.

Ivy Payne's children were all out at the front of the road; only Jeanette came across crying for her Mammy, and Clara placed an arm around her waist and told her that her Mammy was sure to come back just now.

For the rest of the afternoon the Walcotts remained at their front window. The rest of the yard population kept drifting in and out, standing around with the growing number of people gathered on the grassy sides of the road to watch the looters going by, or simply to stare at the unruly billowings of smoke and flames licking the skies.

'Guianese people really stupid,' observed Dinah contemptuously, her hair in brown paper screws. 'Look how they burning down their own country, and look at this fool . . .' she continued, referring to Crazy-Mannie, the black man who spent most of his time sitting on a box outside the rumshop, plucking out his eyebrows.

Crazy-Mannie kept coming and going, giving everyone a running commentary on what was happening downtown.

'Santos gone,' he announced in a loud dramatic voice, throwing up his hands in the air.

Fifteen minutes later he returned. 'Kirpilany gonnnne . . . Singh and Brothers gonnnnne . . . Bookers gonnnne' – gonnnne, meaning under fire, and at the pronouncement of each 'gonnnne' a wave of mounting murmurings came from the watching people.

The people cheered as a short wiry man, his dark face swimming in sweat, came by, pushing a medium-sized refrigerator laid across the handle bar of his bicycle.

'Today is black people birthday,' he called out, the muscles in his arms steeling against any shift in his luxurious burden. Others followed with bolts of cloth on their heads, chairs, tables, stereo sets.

Dinah wanted to go out to see some of the action in the streets but Clara was adamant. She could have insisted, but seeing the anxiety on her mother's face she gave a resigned but not unhappy suck-teeth and retired to bed with a book, getting up every once in a while to see the progress of the flames, sparing a thought for Hartley and what he might be doing.

In spite of the upheaval, there was a quality of unreality about the hot, almost oppressively bright afternoon, like something out of a Western film, the way the sky was calmly receiving the growing procession of flames.

'Aiee,' said Archie, as he watched more and more people

deserting the sides of the road to join the crowds sweeping downtown for a share in the goodies. 'Well, I choose a bad time to move to this place,' he admitted to Clara, rubbing his forehead, 'I tell you, when the British pull out of here, it's going to be hell to pay.'

'The British, the British,' muttered Dinah inside, 'he's a real colonialist.'

There is something holy about Georgetown at dusk. The Atlantic curling the shoreline, brown and laced with foam; further out, rough and glowing faintly in the last rays of the afternoon sunlight. The Atlantic, vast and overwhelming, but so native, as if it belongs to Guiana alone. The Atlantic, kept out by the solid grey sea wall where the Georgetown people love to meet. The shadow of the ocean and the shield of the wall make a perfect foil for lovers locked below. At the edge of the jetty a man throwing his castnet to the deceptively calm water below is framed against the horizon and a little further inland, the white cathedral and the wooden houses cast peaceful shadows on to the avenues and streets, the trade winds gentle at this hour.

Dusk tonight over the city of wood is all dancing, orange-black flames, billowing like a biblical catastrophe.

Some of the Charlestown people were already fetching their belongings out on to the street in a bid to save something in case the fires reached them.

Archie, who regarded most of them as foolish people out to dramatise every situation, paid no attention to his children's pleas to let them start fetching out their own furniture.

'The big heavy piano alone gun take an age to lift out,' said Gem in despair. 'Is what we waiting for?' The earlier excitement had long receded, leaving an icy coldness in her hands. She and Anthony kept up their vigil at the window, counting all the fires they could see, making guesses as to how close they were, how long before reaching their house. 'That one look like it by the jail now,' said little Anthony, 'three more corners and then is our house.'

They had to keep calm, Archie thought, as he switched back on the radio. A reporter was describing the worst of all the fires which began at a Drug Company on Lombard Street and was sweeping everything in its wake. The work stoppage at the electricity company meant that the mains were without water and the fire brigades were grappling with water pumps in the nearby canals.

Archie listened to the crackling explosions in the background as the reporter described the exquisite colours of the flames caused by the chemicals, the blues, the greens, the pinks.

Then he heard a sound coming from under the house and rushed to the back window. Two figures were fetching some heavy equipment through his backgate. It was Marcus and Vibert, taking a short cut with the afternoon's spoils. Ivy had already come back and Clara had sent Jeanette over.

'Well, that is what I call presumption to its height, man,' he said to Clara, 'coming through my yard with stolen goods. I don't know how people could be so barefaced.'

'Archie, I have more to think about than people fetching things through yard,' cried Clara vexedly.

Then Mohabir came on the air. He said he had asked the Governor to send for British troops but that Governor Rothschild had only sent a cable, telling them to be on standby.

Clara, who no longer worried to hide her fear from the children, said, 'But is what the hell he waiting for, for the whole blasted place to burn down? And we can't even see Conrad,' she added, thinking how much they could all do with his dangerous, reassuring presence.

They had forgotten all about Mrs Lall. The children giggled nervously as her short, stout frame came swiftly and silently into the yard, carrying a brown bag stuffed with clothes. Her voice floated up before her thinly as she reached the steps, 'Nabe nabe.'

106

Mrs Lall was shaking her head from side to side when they opened the door for her.

She looked shorter and older under the bright fluorescent light. Her thin mouth which gave her a sneering appearance merely looked pathetic now and she seemed like a woman about to make some desperate move. 'Teacha Teacha,' she said to Archie, holding on to the back of a chair to support herself.

Archie, who responded to names of that nature, softened a bit, but his voice when it came was still matter-of-fact, 'So you're here,' he said, eyeing her brown bag suspiciously. 'Well, we have to wait and see what happens. This is what Guiana has come to.'

'I love black people,' wailed Mrs Lall, clutching at Clara's hand distractedly, 'I really love dose people.'

'Don't distress yourself too much, Mrs Lall,' said Clara, 'All we can do is leave everything in God's hands.'

As soon as Archie went inside Mrs Lall began to plead, 'Owh nabe, I-yuh must tek me with I-yuh when you going, me na go give no trouble.'

'We don't know what we doing yet, nabe,' said Clara.

But around eight o'clock it was decided that Dinah and the children should spend the night at their Cousin Wilma in Agricola, a small village on the East Bank, just outside Georgetown. Dinah could be depended on to get them there safely.

You, Dinah and Anthony walk quickly, taking short cuts through some of the quieter back streets. Groups of people still standing about the roads gazing up at the skies. As you walk you keep looking back at the skies too, counting all the orange blazes like billowing bottle lamps in the sky. You feel like a girl in one of those schoolgirl comics. A heroine looking back at her city in ruins.

As you walk, with a bag of clothes hanging from your shoulder, nothing tell you that you'd ever see your home again. The rocking chair, the settee, the big piano, the small coconut palm at the front of the yard and that purple plant, the gooseberry tree. All would be gone, maybe the entire Charlestown yard, nothing remaining in the morning but the blackened earth. But you feel calm. Full of a calm, frightened excitement.

'If the worst comes to the worst,' Dinah say, 'Mummy and Daddy will follow, bringing Mrs Lall, I suppose.'

13

Although she had received no word about their coming, Cousin Wilma, who was a distant cousin, welcomed them as if she'd been expecting them all afternoon. She lived at the end of a long dark yard in a small house, almost hidden by a tremendous guenip tree which seemed to be guarding the house in its immense shadow.

Cousin Wilma, who was in her mid-forties and due to be married soon, was a seamstress, a plump, light brown woman with wavy hair and eyes that spoke of many calamities. Within the last week a zinc sheet had come off her kitchen roof, she had twisted her ankle and her bicycle was stolen. 'I don't know, it just seem to be my luck,' she would say.

Her house, which gave off an earthy, musty scent was strewn with ends of cloth, strips of blue, patches of green and flowered triangles. Her bed was covered with half-finished dresses, fashion books and new, folded materials as yet untouched by her femininely fashioning hands. She could never complete anything in time though, so the people who gave her work usually lied that they needed the particular dress or skirt a day or two before they actually did. In any case, they still had to undergo hours of sulky waiting while she stitched, pinned and hemmed, and related the incident that had prevented her from completing it.

Tonight she was thirsty for news of the fire which she couldn't see because of the big factory buildings at the head of the main road. Dinah told her all about it and she responded, 'But is whuh we coming to nuh,' in her soft, rounded voice which flowed between English and Creole, as the mood swayed her.

She cleared the bed by gathering everything up and dropping it loosely into a sheet on the floor. Dinah and Gem could sleep with her on the bed and Anthony on the carpet in the corner. She wasn't making her own bridal dress, she said, because it was unlucky for a bride to do that. It was a good thing she had some bakes left back. She made them some Ovaltine to go with the bakes and they devoured them hungrily.

Then she went on talking. She needed reassurance about marrying James. She didn't know whether she was doing the right thing at her age. She had met him one afternoon as she was crossing a street in Georgetown. He was driving his car and had pulled up to let her pass, then he had turned around and offered her a lift. Dinah had met him only once and thought he was horrible, a big vulgar-looking man of about sixty with flat, squashy lips in a sour, pompous face. But she didn't say any of these things. Instead she just listened and smiled as if this marriage was going to be the most natural and beautiful thing. Cousin Wilma's house seemed miles away from the frantic burning world she had left an hour ago.

Archie, Clara and Mrs Lall kept their vigil. The fires did seem to be looking more under control and at about five o'clock the next morning the British troops arrived. The Governor had sent another cable ordering them in.

As the skies gave way to greyish dawn, Mrs Lall slowly made her way back to her own home. She didn't look relieved but merely like one whose fate had been suspended.

110

Although they hadn't slept a wink, on the morning after the fires both Clara and Archie felt in lighter spirits. Perhaps it was the knowledge of the sober-looking British soldiers in the country.

With a calm air of propriety the troops were now guarding the charred, smoking ruins around the city which they had already cordoned off – what was left of big department stores and shops and buildings. It would take at least a week before anyone could venture to search among the twisted black wreckage of mattress springs and bicycle frames, chromium tables and steel chests and other red hot junk – iron and black metal skeletons, the only survivors of a death by fire.

Throughout the week people left their homes specifically to see the sight, standing around in chastened little crowds, staring in awe at the disfigurements. Staring too at the green-clad soldiers whose presence, more than anything, said that what had happened was a really big thing.

The police began their laborious and almost fruitless task of searching for stolen goods, prising up the floor boards of the homes of people whom they suspected. But everything, it seemed, was too well buried or hidden. A curfew too came into being every night from ten.

But in spite of everything, things began to resume a more normal rhythm. Many modifications were made in the budget. The strike was called off. People were going to work again, except for those who had lost their jobs with the fires. Buses were running. Factories were humming.

On Dinah's first morning back after the fires, Hartley came in late and threw down his haversack.

'We never learn. We never learn,' he said in despair at her table. 'This is just what the Americans want. We've played right into their bloody hands. Now we have the British troops to take care of the natives who can't take care of themselves.'

And as the laws of nature would have it, every action has a reaction: so too the coming of the soldiers on the female section of the population. Within a few weeks of their coming soldiers and young women were being married, no less than three or four couples every week in the city's various churches.

The Sunday papers gave their full blessings to these weddings which were seen as a tribute to the beauty of Guianese womanhood. Week after week they carried the smiling photographs of each couple and the accompanying tender story of soldier and local girl who had fallen in love at first sight.

One man boasted how he was able to marry off all his daughters in the space of a few months and more and more people flocked the churches to witness the sight of meek, blond- and dark-haired bridegrooms being whisked away by smiling local girls. A hardy British soldier even managed to drag one of the well-known Georgetown prostitutes to the altar and some of the 'unluckier' women gnashed their teeth, marriage to a white foreigner being synonymous with a life of luxury and ease.

Then there was Cousin Wilma's wedding. It was decided that, since her yard was so long and treacherous and the church in which she was being married was so close to the Walcotts', she should dress from their home.

And though it was the smallest of weddings it seemed that the traditional confusion would still reign. It was a seven o'clock wedding but up to six-thirty the bridal dress hadn't arrived as yet. Clara combed out her hair hurriedly, and started out for the seamstress who lived a ten-minute walk away, leaving Wilma in her underwear on the verge of tears.

She met the seamstress about halfway down the street, a short, dark, god-fearing woman who broke out in cold sweat at the sight of Mrs Walcott. There had been some mishap, she explained in an agonised fashion. She had finished Wilma's dress at twelve o'clock the night before and had it all wrapped up to deliver early this morning. But her eldest daughter, without looking inside the parcel, had handed it to the young boy who had come early this morning to collect his sister's dress. The sister was also going to a wedding. She was on her way to remedy the mishap, she explained, breathing hard, her eyes pleading for understanding. 'For God sake, hurry then,' said Clara, and at these words the seamstress broke into a run.

Back at the Walcotts' house, a group of women were standing at the gate even though nobody knew how they had heard of the wedding. At a quarter to seven a grey car containing Wilma's elderly cousin drove up to the gate and honked twice. He was a small-chested man, dressed in an impressive grey suit with a neatly folded white handkerchief at his breastpocket. Today he was the father giver, and his face reflected the task.

Some of the women who were standing at the head of the bridge went to stare at him through the car window and he regarded them coldly and told the chauffeur to blow his horn again. Gem came running out to tell him that Wilma wasn't ready and that he must come back in about ten minutes. The car drove off with the elderly cousin sitting straight-faced.

At the promptings of the women, Gem explained to them about the dress.

'I don't like the sound of that attall,' a plump woman broke out even before Gem had finished speaking, and they turned to give each other knowing looks.

'Something fishy guying on,' said another woman eagerly and they began to talk among themselves, putting forward their own reasons as to the delay of the dress. All felt that obeah was involved. All sided with the bride.

Meanwhile, Wilma, who had taken Clara's advice on everything, insisted on wearing foundation make-up and rouge and outlining her nicely shaped brows in heavy black pencil, drawing them down in two arcs which immediately gave her a hooded look. But she felt that she needed a new face to cope with the new identity she was going to assume.

Like many Guianese brides, she looked completely different from her usual self. The smooth texture of her still firm cheeks had taken on a putty-like appearance. Her hair, which had been pressed too straight the day before, fell lank and flat around her skull. Her face looked strained from the constriction of the white corset she had struggled into.

At exactly five minutes to seven the grey car with Aunt Wilma's cousin drove up again and honked. The elderly cousin waited for about a minute then hopped out in vexation and said in a trembling voice, 'Doesn't Wilma know the time? It's now,' he said, pausing for effect, 'two minutes to the hour.'

'But is wha is he case?' asked a gruff-voiced woman loudly. 'He en know de woman ent get she frack as yet.'

'Youall don't have anything better to do,' said the cousin, getting back into the car and slamming the door.

'But look de dry up old shrimp,' laughed another woman.

Five minutes later the sweat-covered seamstress came hurrying in. As she passed the bridge one of the women said loudly so that she could hear, 'They trying to stop de woman from getting she man.' The seamstress who felt on the verge of tears herself, silently helped Wilma, who had resigned herself to fate at this stage, into the dress. It was a little tight in the bosom but Clara pressed a prayer book with two long white streamers into Wilma's hand and led her out of the door.

All around Georgetown at this time, there's a rustling among the poorer segments of the population, a burgeoning of new clothes, new shoes, new dresses, new shirts and trousers, nighties and hats: a resurrection of the smaller items looted in the recent fires. People who had been nowhere near the scene of the looting come into little bonanzas through friends of friends, relatives of relatives, and other far-reaching connections.

Deprived little girls are beginning to play around in

114

spanking new dresses; deprived shirt-tail boys in crisp trousers; men and women stepping out in high-priced leather shoes. The clothes are being worn with discretion, as totally new outfits from top to bottom would only arouse suspicion.

Though the bigger luxury goods like fridges and stereos still remain hidden, the smaller items begin to circulate generously, unexpected gifts coming to even those who had condemned the looting.

On Easter Sunday morning blind Mrs Castello, leaning on Mr Castello's arm, stepped out in a pair of bright blue leather wedge-heels which fitted her like a soft glove. Holding on to the pew in church, she sang *Up From the Grave He Arose* in her most soulful of voices. On bended knee she prayed generously, praying not only for her devoted Mr Castello, who had left her by the church door and would later come to collect her, but praying also for the contentious neighbours in the yard, praying for the country ('Lord, stop the strife and troubles and guide us through to peace and harmony'), praying for the gift of her new shoes ('Lord, you don't come but you does send'), Mr Castello himself being blessed with two expensive leather shoes, a left-sided pair, which he mashed down at the heels to accommodate his feet.

These 'godsends' or windfalls extended even to the Walcott household. Clara got some cotton print from one of her cousins, Cousin Lucille, and made from it a puff-sleeved dress for Gem, a shirt for Anthony and housecoat for Dinah. Archie got a box of handkerchiefs, and he considered it best not to question the source as he mopped his brow.

The children were all unbelievably proud of these clothes, even Dinah, old as she was. Lying around in her red-flowered housecoat, she felt as though she was wearing a piece of her country.

Easter Monday. Kite flying time up on the sea wall.
Nothing can stop the kites singing in the skies all around
the sea wall. Not the burnt out fires or the soldiers.
Easter Monday and you, Anthony and Conrad moving
down to the sea wall, the kites, with their green and
yellow bull-wings, already flapping on your backs as you
come nearer and nearer the sea wall, like if they can't
wait to take off in the Atlantic breeze. So much colour
in the skies. You've never seen so much colour in the
skies. Conrad helping Anthony with his kite, Anthony
running, the kite rising, then dipping back to the ground.
Anthony running again and this time the kite zigging
upwards. Now it's your kite. You let out the string, feeling
the kite pulling in the strong wind. See Conrad letting
it go. Feeling it pulling and dancing and dipping, tail
weaving. Then steadying itself and rising, rising, against
the skies with all the other kites. Box kites, singing-
engine kites, pointer-broom kites, newspaper kites, one
so big that four men raising it, and little kites like bright
dresses in the sky. And Conrad tying the twine around
your waist, so both your hands free to eat a ice-cream
cone or anything, and your kite still way up in the skies.

14

Towards the end of May some of the troops began to withdraw, leaving in batches and taking the local brides they had acquired with them.

The weather became very rainy. It wasn't the usual heavy, off and on kind of rain, but a finer, more persistent rain that drugged the senses, making Archie feel more depressed than ever, especially at the sight of water dripping from the charcoal ruins of the city which festered like patches of bad skin.

'Like the rainy season is upon us,' observed Clara, when he came in from his morning routine, leaving his outshapen black umbrella to drip on the front landing outside.

'Ah ha,' he agreed, adding with a sigh, 'looks as if my umbrella is leaving me.'

He took out two large grapefruits and a hand of speckled bananas and placed them on the table. Clara, who had seen him perform this very action many times, suddenly experienced a rush of tenderness at the sight of his mellowed dark brown hands placing the fruits on the table, the familiar expression of martyrdom on his face. She wanted to wipe it away with her hand and hold his frame against hers for a moment, but the years of inhibition outside of the bedroom prevented her.

Instead she got up and went towards the table under the pretext of getting the kitchen knife then as if casually, began to brush the wings of the grey rainflies that had settled on the back of his jacket.

'I've had a bad night last night,' sighed Archie, referring to his sinuses as he lowered himself into his Berbice chair. Little acts like those aroused his self pity. He closed his eyes and leaned back in the chair.

And it went on raining placidly all afternoon, dispelling once again the myth that if rainflies came out before midday the afternoon inevitably would be bright and sunny.

Like most of the land along the coast, the Walcotts' yard was low and within a few days the entire place was flooded. In the back garden the bora vines were sagging badly from the slim poles Archie had stuck in the earth to allow them to climb and the green heads of the calaloo and tomato plants struggled to keep above the brown blanket of water.

The trench running under the front bridge had also risen, covering the sloping grassy parapets and some of the sunken boards on the bridge itself. The passageway was so flooded that the planks he had laid down floated like the survivors of a wreck.

Down at the markets the gutters were also overflowing with soft, swollen mangoes and bananas and empty water coconut shells which soon became infested with mosquito eggs. Everywhere the water gushed and flowed.

Still, the fat East Indian woman who came everyday, selling fish and other greens and fruits, waddled through it like a stoical Buddha, the heavy basket balancing on her head. The sight of her large wet bosom and bleached, ducklike toes disturbed Clara and every day she kept saying the same thing to her, 'Radge, you not afraid you get pneumonia?' At times the sight of her set, wet face was more than Clara could stand and she would insist on her taking a hot cup of tea before moving on.

The lowness of the place was one of the factors Archie had overlooked when buying the house and he lamented not having seen it under rainy conditions. Now he had to pay for it, he thought, going around in his long boots and wearing a trapped expression.

The fact that most of the troops had already left the country also made him feel uneasy as he was certain that everything hadn't abated.

As soon as the weather became dry again he ordered a truckload of compressed tin blocks and two truckloads of heavy lumps of earth to make up his yard.

The loads duly arrived and were dumped at the side of the roadway, in front of his home. And the shirtless boys, or rather, young men who hung out daily under the sandbox tree on the opposite side of the road, nudged one another and looked on.

Archie had intended doing the work himself with the help of his children but this wasn't very practical. In any case, Gem and Anthony, after fetching in a few of the heavy blocks and dragging in bits of earth in old baskets, soon lost interest in their father's project and the work was too much for Archie alone, even though he made a brave start.

So the young men got up and came lazily towards him. There were six of them and they offered to do the job at five dollars a head.

Archie regarded them sceptically, having deplored their idleness, crudeness and indecent manner of dress from the time he had moved into the area. They were always there, sitting under the tree, laughing and interfering with the women going by. They were trying to look earnest now, grinning sheepishly, but Archie could detect the hardness underneath that told him they didn't give a damn about the making-up of his yard.

He wasn't deceived but he gave them the job in the end. Not at five dollars each but at three, which he felt was more than enough. They worked well enough at first, though with much loud talk and banter, but as soon as Archie went in to eat they began to slacken off, laughing and joking among themselves. Archie regarded them from behind the bedroom window curtain. 'They complain about not getting work, but they don't really want to work,' he told his wife angrily, inviting her to come to the window and take a look, 'My people, like they're cursed, man.' Archie clapped his hands at the window, calling, 'Get a move on with it.'

But the lads managed to take all afternoon, and the next morning he had to pay them an extra dollar each to finish off the job which wasn't done to his satisfaction at all.

He was to make that comment, 'My people, like they're cursed, man,' throughout the years in his Princess Street home.

He made it when the little shirt-tail boys tried to walk over the narrow drinking-water pipe that ran alongside his bridge. He made it once when someone picked his pocket. And he made it at weekends when Ivy Payne held her weekly Saturday night dances and Sunday picnics. He had come to dread those weekends with the loud music and rum drinking next door. The music began on Saturday evening and went well into Sunday morning, sometimes past sunrise if the dancers and rum were still around. Then at two on the Sunday afternoon it promptly began again. The political tension and fires had in no way affected the frequency of her parties, it seemed to him.

He still went to church each Sunday and had taken to spending most of the day out, visiting old acquaintances, more than anything in an effort to avoid the noise next door. Clara hardly ever went with him. The effort seemed much harder to make here. He noted this attitude of hers, this lapsing into acceptance of the life. Her ironic smile and shrug, 'What to do? You were the one to buy the house and now we have to make the most of it.'

Clara herself wasn't averse to all the calypsoes and could be heard humming *Bury Me Under the Tray of Dalphoori* or *Love in the Cemetery*.

And the children, they seemed to like them well enough. Gem knew the words of all the latest calypsoes. And didn't he catch Dinah twice, peeping out the small bathroom window, staring at the drunken, amorous scenes next door? Sometimes there were fights and the sounds of breaking bottles and chairs, and twice they had ripped out his paling staves in what he thought was a callous disregard for other people's property.

The next thing you know there's another strike in the country, a general strike. Everybody on strike, your mother say, because the Trade Union people angry with the government about some bill.

Soon everything is scarce. Sugar, milk, rice, flour, cooking oil, kerosene. Soon there are lines all over the place, stringing out like centipedes in front of the barred-up shops with just a narrow gap for the shopkeepers to hand through the parcels. The shopkeepers saying they will close up if people flock them too much.

You stand with your sister in one of these lines, baking in the sun. Waiting patiently for sugar. Sugar is by far the most important thing for you. You can't bear tea without sugar, can't make fudge or sugarcake or anything without it.

In the line the women squash you up with their heavy dampness. Somebody shove from in front and you totter backwards. The same thing happen from behind and this time you're squeezed out of the line. Dinah grab your hand and pulling you back in again.

Around Stabroek Market square people flooding

round the bus station, but the rows of yellow buses not moving. Just standing there, ever since the first day of the strike. But today is different. Today the government got some other drivers to drive the buses, but some of the people won't have any of that. They shout 'Scabs!' and surround the buses, singing, 'Solidarity forever, solidarity forever, solidarity forever, for the union makes us strong.'

You feel fear, excitement, churning inside you, because you know any moment now the police van could round the corner. But this time it doesn't happen.

15

In spite of the strike and the tensions Mrs Ramsammy was determined to have a little something for Deepavali, festival of lights, triumph of good over evil. On the eve of the Hindu festival she invited Clara and Archie over along with some other friends.

From early that morning she had her household busy. Mrs Ramsammy's household was large and she ruled it with a short, sweeping hand. Everyone feared her biting tongue — everyone except her daughter-in-law, a tall, thin girl with slightly protruding eyes.

Mrs Ramsammy filled a number of little clay bowls with oil and her grandchildren swept the entire yard though she always said it was the duty of the tenants downstairs to do so. The house was dusted, furniture pushed aside and rearranged. Later she, her eldest daughter and her daughter-in-law made a silent truce and took to the kitchen.

Usually there were rounds of violent quarrelling between the hot-mouth daughter-in-law, Zabeeda, and her husband's large family. Mrs Ramsammy, who had been hoping for a submissive daughter-in-law, was bitterly disappointed. Whenever her husband tried to beat her, Zabeeda would fight back, her wiry body clawing and scratching. Sometimes she ran out of the house and from the safety of the paling, behind the bread-fruit tree, would hurl abuse at the entire family. This 'busing out never failed to entertain the Charlestown people and win their admiration.

But of late even Mrs Ramsammy seemed to have been drained by her daughter-in-law's nervous energy for these days she merely referred to her as, 'this streak ah misery' while Zabeeda, not to be outdone, could be heard casting remarks about some people whose hands too short to wash they own behinds.

Mrs Ramsammy's hands were short and she had already decided that she had no luck with either daughters or daughters-in-law or, for that matter, sons. Her eldest daughter's husband had died, resulting in her having to come back home with the three children. Her second son was married to Zabeeda and her eldest son, her doctor boy Vishnu, who was in the USA, to crown it all, had married a coloured American girl, a lab. assistant called Brenda, on the last lap of attaining his MD.

Still for Deepavali, festival of goodwill, they worked together in the kitchen, Zabeeda boiling rice in milk with sugar and raisins and making other sweetmeats and Mrs Ramsammy and her daughter doing the main dishes.

And when it was sufficiently dark Mrs Ramsammy, always lamenting the competition that came from the street lights, lit the wicks floating in the little bowls of oil, then she led the way round, dotting the window sills, the steps, the verandah, with the lights.

Shortly after Clara and Archie came over, Clara feeling a bit guilty because she had recently started to take a few things on credit from Mrs Ramsammy who had a grocery section to the rumshop. None of the other guests had arrived and Mrs Ramsammy, fresh in a flowered sari, and her unobtrusive, older-looking husband welcomed them heartily. Since they had never visited the house before Mrs Ramsammy took them on a guided tour, moving in quick little steps. Into her daughter-in-law's bedroom which was painted in deep blue. Into her grandchildren's bedroom, the biggest room in the house, painted pink with freshly made up beds on the floor. Into her own bedroom which was the smallest, lilac in colour and hazy with the smoke of incense.

The living room itself was large with an over-furnished, heavy look even though the glass cabinets were pushed back against the wall to create more space. There were potted plants and gold brocade curtains, tables with ornaments, plastic covered sofas with satin cushions and lots of family photographs on the walls. In one corner was a big table with a huge glass bowl of rum punch and glasses all around it.

From the doorway of the dining room Clara could see children's faces peeping out. Mr Ramsammy pointed out some small figures of Hindu gods which he himself had made from clay and varnished. Then Clara and Archie were given glasses of rum punch and led out to the verandah. Clara was impressed by the neat efficiency of the house, her own lacking that order, and she admired the little Deepavali lights and the plants. The Ramsammys had closed their rumshop for the night and it was fairly cool and quiet, sitting out there with their drinks. Archie was sipping his with restraint because he didn't believe in strong drink.

Mr Ramsammy, who had remained on the verandah with them, took a big gulp at his own drink and began to talk about himself. How he had to leave school when he was eleven to help in the ricefields. How he had acquired what he had today the hard way. 'But I never grudge my children anything,' he said, rubbing the back of his hand across his nose, an irritating habit which he had acquired. Archie was surprised at his talkativeness.

Other guests arrived, a black lawyer and his half-Indian wife, some of the Ramsammys' own relatives and other well-to-do looking people. A band of Indian musicians, all men, also arrived and immediately sat together in a group on the floor.

126

Dinner was served. The big table was cleared of its rum punch and covered with a white table cloth and another table was drawn close by. The tables were laid with plates, knives and forks, hotware dishes of roti and alloo curry and pumpkin and bora stew, other fried vegetables, rice and dhal.

Clara, Archie, the lawyer and his wife and some Indian uncles sat at the big table while the other women guests sat at the smaller one. They were all served with more rum punch, then sweet desserts and Pepsi Cola after. When everyone had eaten, the musicians came to the table.

Later in the evening as the little clay pots were burning low the musicians began to play, sitting on the floor, crashing small but heavy looking cymbals together, and making what Archie considered a deafening noise. But even the noise was not enough to drown out the sudden and unmistakeable boom of a bomb explosion somewhere in the city.

'God bless America,' said the women who were handed the fat brown packages of oatmeal and powdered milk down at the relief kitchens, part of the American government's aid to sustain the families of the striking Georgetown workers.

'The Americans are hypocrites,' said Dinah, combing her hair in front of the mirror, 'they playing they so concerned about the poor people but they're only support- ing the strike because it suits them.'

Clara looked at this daughter of hers. This daughter who looked so strong and capable with her slightly slanting, rebellious eyes. This daughter who had bought her a fridge from her own money, and who had recently taken to making political observations about the world, dismissing nations, as she combed her hair in front of the mirror.

Clara said lamely, 'Girl, you better don't let your father hear you.' More and more these days she found herself acting as mediator between husband and daughter who came into headlong clashes.

'Is all part of bringing down the government,' continued Dinah in the blustering tone she used whenever she made a political observation. 'Divide and rule. Divide and rule. Why the Americans don't give aid to the sugarworkers? Why they're only helping the strikers? It's just to destabilise the country and give the British a good excuse for not granting independence.'

Archie heard her. 'That girl is becoming more and more presumptuous with each passing day,' he said to Clara in parental outrage. 'I don't know where she's picking up her political ideas from but she's heading for a fall.'

If anyone was heading for a fall it didn't look like Dinah, budding with a new revolutionary consciousness, showing a concern for remoulding the world, saying things like: 'Two babies come into the world. Neither ask to be born. Why should one come into a life of riches just because their parents happen to be rich and the other into a life of poverty? Both should have the same chance.'

One afternoon Hartley visited her in a wine-coloured T-shirt and little black beret. Sitting on the settee, waiting for Dinah to come out, he tried to appear nonchalant, picking up a newspaper and pretending to read under Archie's scrutiny.

'I don't want that communist-looking chap back here,' Archie said to his daughter who was inside, pulling on a skirt over her shorts. Dinah merely flounced out of the house with Hartley, supposedly off to her Badminton Club.

'You've seen the chap she's just gone off with?' Archie asked. 'Nothing will convince me that he isn't part of some communist mix up.'

'He's working at her Ministry,' said Clara, trying to treat it mildly. 'She spoke of him before, Hartley, he's suppose to be joining her Badminton Club.'

'Suppose, eh!' said Archie. 'At least you seem to be in the know. She listens to nothing I say these days. In fact, she seem to get a delight out of contradicting everything I say.'

'Archie, she's at an age when she's forming her own ideas. You shouldn't take everything she say so seriously.'

'Forming her own ideas,' said Archie, 'she's just impressionable, headstrong and downright rude.'

Archie always remembered how Dinah had demanded the right to collect her own salary just two years after she had started teaching. She was sixteen at the time. He had been collecting her salary for the first two years of teaching and giving her back what he thought was 'a suitable sum'. But from the set of her face at sixteen he knew he had little choice but to let her receive her own pay packet.

'She thinks she playing baby-party,' he went on, 'full of big words these days, mixing with all kinds of radical-looking people. Take care when she gets burnt is a different story.'

'Dinah can take care of herself,' said Clara with conviction, even though Hartley wasn't quite how she had imagined him. 'She said he was just a friend.'

'Friend,' Archie snorted. He always felt that his wife's easy upbringing was responsible for a 'multitude of sins'. The careless way she kept the home, the almost irresponsible freedom she allowed the children.

'Our children all have their own different little personalities,' said Clara, trying to steer Archie on to lighter pastures.

'Anthony is so sensitive. You remember the time we had his hair cut. He was five. He gathered all his locks together on that sheet of newspaper, bringing them for me to see. "All mih nice nice hair gone, Mummy," he said, standing before me with his little shorn head. I felt so sorry I had it cut.

'Gem,' Clara went on with indulgent pride, 'has such an innocent look, but people better not take her for a fool. That little girl does come up with some things. She's really imaginative. I was reading a composition in her exercise book the other day. And she's tough too. Could stand up for herself.'

Archie listened as his wife played with the different qualities of their children, something she did from time to time as if she really found it fascinating, dwelling on the little idiosyncrasies of each, smiling romantically.

Clara didn't touch on Dinah, however, for Archie's sake, though she still felt deep down inside that Dinah was going to be 'somebody'.

Everybody at home now, your brother, sister, Lurleena, all the other children in the yard. You don't mind the strike, because no school. Your school's being used as one of the relief kitchens by the Christian Crusade for sharing out free meals to the children of the workers on strike. Dinah say that the US handing out the money for the food because they want the government out. But your mother wouldn't dream of sending you for a free meal. Every day you and Lurleena watch the other children coming back, biting into big rolls with things like ham and cheese inside. Every afternoon you listen for the voice of the Trade Union president on the radio. You're anxious to hear his last words after the singing of solidarity forever. It's always the same; 'The strike continues.' You want the strike to continue. Your heart lift at the words. No school.

16

Conrad came often these days, rocking Gem on his lap and recalling the time when the British suspended the constitution, a time that gave birth to poems of resistance and saw the imprisonment of opponents to the colonial regime. 'Those were times,' he said, warming to his pet subject, 'I can't forget the Governor voice on the radio: "Her Majesty's government has decided that the constitution of British Guiana must be suspended to prevent communist subversion." That was a hell of a time, buddy. The early fifties.'

'I remember,' Archie said, regarding Conrad from the comfort of his Berbice chair. 'I had just moved to Highdam. I often think how the course of this country's history would have changed if that suspension didn't happen.'

Conrad, sensing Archie's old fear of communism, began to relish the effect this kind of conversation had on him. 'Everything then was a red plot,' he went on in sounds of choking laughter. 'I was working under old Headley, police chief at the time. The force was in a mass of confusion. Old Headley reported a plot to burn down Georgetown to the Colonial Office. It was a red plot, they said. Everything was red. What a laugh!

'I can't forget poor Mrs De Silva. The lady was terrified out of her skin. "Oh God, Conrad come quick. I don't know what to do. My servant gone mad, taking over my house, saying that is her house now because the government promise to take away the houses from the rich people and give them to the poor." Calm down, woman, I said. I had just come in from work, I was still wearing my CID clothes, and Archie boy, if you hear poor Mrs De Silva babbling away as we walk down to her house on Brickdam. One of these elegant colonial houses. And there was this buxom black woman standing at the front window.

'"What nonsense is this?" I bellowed, stomping up the stairs. If you see the woman run. Picked up her bags and was out the house quick time. I was tickled pink. Poor Mrs De Silva believed in me like the Virgin Mary after. After that she couldn't do enough for me. "Oh Conrad, you must come and have dinner with us this evening,"' he said, mimicking her in a high simpering voice, '"Oh Conrad, I must see you to discuss something very important." Turned out that her niece Alica was pregnant. A quiet mouse of a girl but quite a nice child. She was only about eighteen at the time. Grew up with Mrs De Silva. Her mother died when she was very young. You could imagine the state Mrs De Silva was in when she found out. Alica pregnant! If she could have dropped dead I suppose she would. Wouldn't say a word to Alica for weeks. In the end the poor child moved out to live with a cousin on Hadfield Street. The next time I saw her she had this bundle in her arms. A baby girl called Isadora, of all things, a tiny little wrinkled thing like a raisin.

'Next thing you know I'm Isadora's babysitter. The mother wanted to take evening lessons in shorthand and typing so I went down there in the evenings to help her. The amazing thing is that Isadora became more attached to me than to her own mother. If you see the little thing clinging to me when I'm handing her back to her mother . . . Oh well, the mother is now married and has another child.'

Archie seized the opportunity to interrupt. 'That woman has no regard for Sunday,' he said, referring to Ivy Payne who has just put on her dukebox, playing Sparrow's

'May-May – Making love one day with a girl they calling May-May. Making love one day with a girl they calling May-May. I pick up May-May by de railway . . .'

'This is the sort of thing I have to put up with every day,' he added as the calypso got louder, 'and the thing is she chooses all the vulgar tunes, none of the nice pieces.'

'I know, old boy. They're from a different class,' said Conrad soothingly.

'But I can't understand why she has to play it so loud, and it doesn't seem to affect the others,' Archie glanced around to see if Clara was nearby.

'Conrad, you going to hear Atwell tonight?' Clara came in with a wicked glint in her eyes.

'I'll probably give it a look-in on my way home,' replied Conrad, adding, 'Mind you, he don't need me at his meetings. He got enough black people to go and hear him, even though some of them don't understand a word he saying. But they fall for the big words. You should hear them clap. Our people love big words, man. The man is a modern-day Prophet Wills. When Prophet Wills find two boys fighting he'll take them to the mother and say, "Madam, I've found your waifs engaging in a pugilistic encounter."'

'Conrad, you always,' laughed Clara.

Archie grinned, his eyes crinkling.

Cousin Wilma came one afternoon to tell Clara how married life was treating her. 'Girl, I come to de conclusion that dat man head ent good. Just the other day I roast some pork, and me with me stupid self go and ask de man if it roast to his approval. Girl, who tell me to ask nuh? De man carry on at a rate, "Woman, you asking me if pork roast to my approval? You think is today I eating roast pork? All dis fuss bout lil roast pork. I been eating roast pork since before you beena wear drawers." Tell me if the man is not a ignorant ass?'

Clara shook with laughter.

'But wait nuh. I ent finish yet,' Cousin Wilma, went on. 'What you think de man do? De man pick up me nice nice plate of roast pork and dash it through the window to de cat. Hear he, "If you don't believe I been eating roast pork since before you beena wear drawers, well I gon show you." Girl, I had a mind to take de same plate and hit he cross he head, but I just put on me clothes and go out de house. And to think before we was married de man was acting so nice. But you know what old people say. You never know where house leaking till you live in it.'

Every morning you wake to eat fried plantain because
you can't get any bread to buy and drink a little
aerated drink because no milk for tea. Every midday
you eat the same thing, callaloo cook-up rice with
shrimps. Sometimes your father manage to get a big
tin of salt-biscuits, through one of his old East Indian
pupils, and some rice. Then he would bring it home
with a half weary-weary, half-pleased kind of look,
saying: 'Youall try and make it last a long time.'
Sometimes when you get milk you encourage
Lurleena to steal her grandmother sugar to make fudge
at your place. When her grandmother find out, she'd
scream at you, 'You, Gem, you're the one
encouraging Lurleena in all this nonsense, and sugar
so hard to get.'

17

No one knew how the beatings and killings started or who really started them first. The Indians blamed the black people. The black people blamed the Indians. And years later, when it was all over, both races liked to pretend that it had never happened, or that it was some kind of dream ghost, best laid to peace and forgotten forever.

Clara remembered the distinct foreboding she felt that morning when she picked up the newspapers and read about the unidentified body of a black man who was found at the back of the ricefields near Skeldon. Maybe it was because the story was only given three paragraphs and wasn't accompanied by a photograph that it set her imagination working – returning again and again to a vision of a slightly swollen, mud-dried corpse on this the thirtieth day of the general strike.

The woman ran as if all the devils of hell pursued her, her long black hair dancing like fine shreds of elastic about her face, clouding her eyes, almost making her trip. But she regained her balance and went on running in desperation, her bamboo basket swinging frantically on her arm, spilling a trail of green mangoes, tomatoes, bhaji, limes, dunks, hearing her own heart thumping, hearing her own breath rasping, knowing that any moment her slender brown legs could collapse from the effort.

Behind they pursued her like a pack of hounds, bicycle wheels in unison, pressing hard, doubled over the bicycle handles – a gang of twelve, fourteen, young men, shirts knotted at navels to expose hard, shiny black chests, faces gleaming with sweat and glee. What a laugh. They'll frighten the life out of this coolie bitch. Teach her a lesson. Frighten the bitch.

· 'Take her boys. Take her,' they cry hoarsely, bicycle wheels pressing hard behind her, laughing, 'Take her boys, take her.'

At her front window Clara watched the scene, hardly believing her eyes. Watched the woman running and running. Watched her stumbling across the bridge that led to her gate. Somehow managing to open the gate. Somehow getting up the stairs, opening her front door and falling inside.

Clara watched the boys, young men, doubled over their bicycles, laughing as they rode away into the hot morning sunshine.

Later that night, in another part of the city, a man tottered out of a rumshop and began his zig-zag way along the pavement that led to his Sussex Street home. A thin, battered looking figure with a dirty Pepsi Cola cap on his head. From a gateway, two young men suddenly emerged and planted themselves across his path, bringing him to a staggering halt.

The man began to smile foolishly, swaying in his stance. The young men scrutinised his face, smelling the rum on his breath, taking in the weather-beaten face, the spit at the sides of his mouth, the features they couldn't quite place.

Realisation beginning to dawn, the man whipped off his cap to reveal his wavy, slightly crinkly hair: 'Dougla . . .

dougla . . .' he stammered, pointing to his hair which indicated that he was a mixture of African and East Indian.

'Dougla, eh,' sneered one of the young men, giving him a knuckle across the mouth. 'Dougla. Well we going beat de coolie out ah yuh dougla rass.'

The man staggered backwards and fell with a muted thud on to the pavement.

Clara wasn't prepared for it. Couldn't accept it or comprehend. The fires and the looting, yes. But not the killing and battering.

Everyday the newspapers began to carry graphic pictures of all the murders. All the grisly details splashed across the pages: The body of a black man who was dragged from a hire-car and hacked to death in some East Indian village. The body of an Indian man floating in a trench in the city.

Clara, protectress of human life that she was, recoiled from the brutality and she told Archie that she couldn't see or understand how one person could kill another, merely on the grounds of race, how they could work up enough hatred.

And Archie, who believed that people were capable of anything, said, 'Well, you're very naive when it comes to certain matters.'

'Naive?' said Clara. 'I bet you if men used to bring children into this world, they would have more respect for human life.'

This was a blessed country, thought Clara as she played the piano. A firm fertile green country, the only inkling of a threat being maybe the Atlantic pounding away along the coast. Things happened in the far off countries. The hurricanes, the wars, the earthquakes, the famine. This place was a piece of paradise on earth.

'Oh I care not that others rave over fair lands afar
I care not that their wealth be great
their sceneries be grand
for none so fair as can compare
with mine own native land . . .'

she sang, fingers rippling the piano keys.

Archie allowed her nostalgia to wash over him. He didn't tell Clara how shocked he was the other afternoon when he went to visit an old friend at the Georgetown Hospital, how the ambulances kept arriving all the time, bringing in people from all parts of the country, shot, butchered or beaten. How the whole place was pervaded by the fresh, heavy odour of death. He had hurried away from the hospital. Hurried home, more out of an instinctive desire to put as much distance between himself and the sights he'd seen than to get off the streets before the eight o'clock curfew began.

One night just as Clara had drifted into sleep, she heard the hoarse, persistent voice of Ivy Payne breaking through her dreamy unconsciousness. 'Mrs Walcott, Mrs Walcott.'

Clara jumped out of bed and stumbled to the back window, Archie behind her. Ivy was leaning on the little front porch of her house in her nightdress.

'I just get the news from Marcus,' she said. 'They planning to burn out the Ramsammys tonight, an' I warning the yard.'

Though it was after midnight and everyone had turned in, the entire yard was astir within a few minutes, lights coming on in all the different households, including Miss Sheila's little house at the end. For if the Ramsammys were burnt out, everyone knew that the entire yard of close wooden houses would be gone, especially with all the rum and spirits around.

In no time Ivy's children were dressed in their yard clothes and sitting out on the front steps, prepared for any eventuality.

The Ramsammys' big house was ablaze with lights and the entire family was sitting with their mostly black tenants who lived in the little cubby holes below. The tenants had helped them to search all around the building, under the

140

low space between the ground and flooring, but they hadn't found anything. A shop similar to theirs had been burnt down just a few nights ago, the fire started by ricebags soaked in petrol and pushed under the building.

Someone said that the Ramsammys had sent for the police, but everyone doubted that the police would come, being too busy to respond to every rumour.

Clara's children woke of their own accord, Dinah first, then Gem and Anthony. Gem was wearing one of her mother's old dresses to sleep in and Clara pulled her away from the window, telling her to go back to bed.

But the excitement tinged with fear kept the children's eyes open.

'Mrs Lall like she coming,' reported Gem, who was back at the window. 'Coming with her bag and baggage to boot.'

'Stop laughing and remove from that window, girl,' ordered Archie. 'This is no time to laugh.'

'Owh nabe, but is wha happening now nuh?' droned Mrs Lall.

That night the Charlestown yard kept vigil with the Ramsammys, who shared out Pepsi Cola and sweet biscuits to keep the wind out of the stomachs.

But it was not until dawn that people ventured back to their beds. Gem sneaked into Dinah's bed and was surprised when Dinah placed an arm around her and said, 'Look,' pointing through the open window to a reddish-looking star in the early morning sky.

You know that something's happening. Happening
within people. Changing them. Making them become
cruel. Every day in the papers you see the pictures, hear
the radio. You see the white soldiers walking in groups
along the pavements. Everybody must be off the
streets by eight o'clock.

Yesterday somehow you were trapped on the
pavement in front of the rumshop. Trapped inside a
thick net of human bodies. What you were doing
there. What they were doing there, you didn't even
know. When the explosion went off it felt as if it gone
right through your own heart, sending you bolting,
crashing along the narrow back passageway, sinking
on to the steps of your own house. But even there you
weren't safe. The teargas fumes pursued you, stifling,
choking and burning. Water, you had to get water.
You dashed upstairs, grabbing the first piece of cloth
within reach and stumbling to the bathroom, soaking
the cloth in water and pressing it to your face,
bending over the bathtub and burying your whole face
beneath the cool surface.

And one night you wake up because you can hear

Mrs Payne screaming a dull kind of scream. You jump out of bed and shake Anthony. Your mother, father and Dinah are all leaning through the back window.

'What happen, Mummy? What happen?'

'Oh God, I think is Vibert.'

You squeeze your head between your mother and Dinah.

The passageway is dark, full of strange moving shadows and voices. Then someone, you think is Stella, come running down the steps, 'They stab-up me brother. They stab-up me brother.'

'Archie, I think I better go over,' your mother say, moving away from the window to get change.

The next thing, you, Dinah and your mother standing with the other people around Vibert, lying halfway in the passageway, a pillow pushed under his head, his hands lying down limp. But you can hardly see his face or the blood seeping through the sheet which the men stuffed up under his shirt.

Everything is confused.

You hear your mother saying, 'You must get him to hospital.'

'But is why they bring he here?' someone ask.

'The man have go get to hospital fast.'

'They couldn't get a car to take him to hospital so they put him on a bicycle and bring him here.'

'But is how it happen?' Voices getting low. Ivy running back out with some more cloth.

'They seh a bomb explode in he hand.'

'The boy keeping bad company.'

You could see your father standing at the back uncertainly.

You hear Mrs Payne saying in a broken voice, 'Boy, is which party you playing stooge for? Boy, if you father was alive today. You breaking mih heart, boy.'

18

Long days of violence and the general strike. The sun treading its hot slow way across the skies. Rubbish, which had been piling up in the city for weeks, beginning to smell in the heat. Archie having to burn theirs in a quiet corner of the back garden behind the gooseberry tree. The relief kitchens sharing out their daily free meals and weekly brown packages. And the Georgetown workers still spending a lot of their time blocking the entrances to their workplaces so that no one with the inclination to work could get in. The police, who had to do their duty, making sudden swoops on them, lifting some bodily into trucks and dumping them in another part of the city – all very ineffective as the strikers soon made their way back again.

Most of the shops claimed to have run out of supplies and shut their doors completely, but quite a few made short surprise openings which the people, ever alert, took advantage of.

In a bid to get some more ration, Clara paid off the Chinese man from the extra housekeeping money that Archie had no choice but to give her. These days there were half-moon shadows beneath her eyes as a result of the snatches of sleep caught between the long listening.

The tit-for-tat mentality between the East Indians and blacks left her feeling heavy rather than frightened.

With an air of tense lassitude she turned the pages of a woman's weekly, vaguely absorbing bits of the romantic encounters of a young English girl in Africa, the rest of her waiting for the reverberating sound of a bomb explosion or a voice calling from across the paling, bringing the details of some gruesome happening, like the launch full of black people blown to bits on the Demerara River.

Around this time cousin Lionel paid a visit. A more thoughtful, less smiling Lionel. 'I done with politics, man,' he told Archie. 'Is a dirty game. Now I hearing that they got my name on a hit list. I never done anybody anything in my life. I think is time for me and the family to get out of this place, boy. Canada. We thinking of moving to Canada.'

Archie didn't really believe him about the hit list, but after Lionel left he still said, 'Hit list. Why is he coming here if his name on a hit list?'

Meanwhile, through it all Conrad kept coming and going, khaki shorts clad, his bony, brown legs taking long, unconcerned strides through the streets of Georgetown, his .38 revolver stuck deep in his back pocket, his monocled eye resting with wry amusement upon some passerby, his head full of political history and know-how, but still maintaining that secrecy about himself.

Not even Archie knew if Conrad ever really voted, or even his date of birth, or what he had done with his sexual energy over the years.

But everyone knew that he was devoted to his mother, a small, frail, dusty-coloured woman of seventy-three whom he called Maudy. Maudy, with her light grey plaits pinned above her head, kept a parrot and a cat who had learnt to tolerate each other after years of cat-spitting and parrot-backchatting. But most of her time was still occupied with thoughts of her only son, Conrad.

Conrad and his mother lived in a sparsely furnished

cottage on Evans Street, and despite the fact that Conrad slept with his revolver not too far from his pillow, his mother lived in constant fear of thieves breaking into the house. Whenever Conrad came home in the evenings, he had to whistle as he turned the key in the lock so that his mother would know it was him.

Conrad had come up with the idea of running electric wires along every window in the house, so that anyone attempting to enter by that means would be electrocuted. But his mother felt that was going too far – in any case, she herself was bound to forget and hold the wires.

The house had two bedrooms but they shared one, with two cots resting on opposite sides of the walls. The other bedroom Conrad used as a study with his books and photographs, and he was fond of converting their bathroom into a darkroom and mixing his chemicals in the sink.

Ever since Conrad's father had died twenty-five years ago, his mother had never seen a doctor. Conrad didn't believe in doctors. He treated all her ailments from constipation to diarrhoea, from ague to high blood pressure. Like everything that Conrad ever did, his battle with his mother's high blood pressure over the years was a thorough one. He had eliminated salt, meat and fat from her diet and made her drink large quantities of green papaw water which he got from boiling green papaws and storing the water in bottles.

His mother saw nothing strange in their lifestyle, and Conrad enjoyed the stares and whispers of their Portuguese neighbours as he pegged his underwear, along with his mother's, on the clothesline under the house.

But though she had been taking the green papaw water it so happened that, on the day following a bomb blast at a garment factory, Conrad's mother took to her bed with a strange sensation in her head.

When Conrad came in from work that evening he found her lying in a state of coma on the bed, the left side of her mouth twisted, her arm hanging limply to one side. Conrad

146

doubled up on the bed beside her, squeezing the hollow of her cheeks and pressing her wrists. He blamed himself for allowing it to happen, certain that she hadn't taken her water. If he had been there this wouldn't have happened.

On the third day following the attack, Conrad's mother died.

He was inconsolable.

The tin of glucose which he had bought stood on the table by her bedside, untouched. So too the bunch of coconuts lying on the floor, their tops beginning to turn greyish brown. She hadn't been able to take anything, not even the water Conrad had held to her lips, his arms cradling her back.

On the morning after her death Conrad moved like a sleepwalker. He went down to the funeral parlour and told the man there that he wanted a coffin and hearse to convey the body the next day. The fact that the gravediggers were on strike was no problem. He would empty the remains of his father's tomb and seal it back up himself, after laying his mother to rest. No, he didn't want any cars to hire as there would be nobody there except himself.

By midday Conrad was hacking away at the entrance of his father's tomb, overgrown by stunted shrubs and glazed by heat. As he worked, he was struck by the homes we give them – the architecture of the dead, doomed to an airless existence.

By the afternoon it was raining slightly. A good omen. And Conrad took out his mother's favourite blue dress and dressed her in it.

But Vibert didn't die. Someone else die. Someone
you didn't expect to die at all. And this time it's your
own mother shaking you awake. Shaking Anthony
too. 'Quick, get up and put on your clothes.'

Dazed, and Anthony even more dazed, you go
outside. But in a few moments you're wide awake and
in a few moments you feel as if your heart is going to
burst. Nothing can stop it from bursting now. Not the
people outside filling the night, thick and soft, or the
red bursts of flames coming from the house two doors
away on the opposite side. Nor your father's drawn
face. Nor your mother's, looking almost as if she was a
different woman, her hair crumpled and loosed out,
her hands shaking each time she tried to pick
anything up. And you don't even see Mrs Lall sitting
in the corner. Don't recognise her at all.

And you're afraid to ask. Afraid to ask whose house
it is. Because you think you know.

Standing at the back of the crowds outside, near the
edge of your own bridge, with the night air feeling
almost cold and then hot on your face, you could see the
flames jumping into the air. And you could see the house

you knew it would be. The house you've been into many times to borrow or exchange books with Teddy.

Your mother and father and sister and brother are standing with you and the crowd is hushed. Suddenly the crowd roaring and people shouting, 'Yes, jump, jump.'

You can't see but you hear it's one of Teddy's big sisters, people telling her to jump from the top bedroom window. Then you begin to cry. You hear the noise of the fire-engine and your father saying, 'Why do they always take so long to come?'

And you can't remember much else after that. At times when something too terrible is happening, your mind or your heart don't want to believe it and so you let everything become hazy and not real. Teddy and all his seven brothers and sisters burning to death and his mother and father. Only the one sister who jumped, escaping.

And the next morning you're surprised to see that the sun still shining. You remember everything now, everything coming back.

Outside, the street still full of people, coming and going or just standing around, gazing at the still burning ruins, talking in low voices.

Why they do it? Who do it? You don't know.

'You wouldn't understand,' your mother tell you. 'It's political.'

And at the breakfast table Anthony looking down at his plate without saying anything. You know that something blocking his throat like a lump, so that he can't eat or swallow anything. Suddenly, he get up from the table and run inside. You run after him and see him lock himself inside the toilet.

'Who would have thought that poor little Teddy would make the news on the BBC,' your mother say in a strange voice as she listen to the World News that morning.

149

19

PR. All the talk now is of PR, the new plan by the British to introduce Proportional Representation into the next elections, less than twelve months away.

As Mohabir begins to agitate over PR, rightly suspecting that it would work to his disadvantage, Conrad who has stayed away for some time following his mother's death, begins to visit again.

Still a little hurt that Conrad didn't tell her anything until after the funeral, Clara treats him coolly. But Gem is as welcoming as ever, nestling in his lap.

Conrad looks a little more bearded and gaunt. 'The East Indians raising holy hell about this PR,' he says to Archie. 'I suppose you have to hand it to the British. They seem to have a plaster for every sore,' Conrad says it a little tiredly, but not without his usual irony. 'I don't think Mohabir expected them to come up with this move.'

But Archie's thoughts are upon putting up their house for sale. Having decided on that course, he spends a lot of his time surveying the neat white house with its paling and back garden, flowering shrubs and coconut palm, trying to turn his thoughts away from political troubles to a quieter environment.

At night Clara's fingers instinctively seek out the root of pain between his brows. Sometimes gently rubbing the flat muscle round and round. Sometimes moving downwards to that other root. Staking a womanly claim of desire.

And one afternoon towards the end of September, who should come down from Highdam in hire-car to see Clara? Except for a few more threads of grey in her hair, visible from under her headtie, Rose was same old Rose, big in a flowered green dress, walking with a bag half-full of rice and mangoes for the family, and some 'bush' for Clara.

When Clara opened the door to her rapping, she gasped, 'Rose! Tell me if I seeing right?'

'Clara,' moaned Rose, dropping her bag. The two women folded each other. After a while, Rose, still holding Clara by the arm, held her off a little and said, 'Let me look at you, girl.'

'Rose,' said Clara again in amazement. 'What you doing here, girl?'

'I need a reason to come and see you?' Rose demanded indignantly.

As Rose settled herself back on the settee, Clara watched the face of her friend, the still finely smooth dark skin, damp from the exertions of travel and the hot afternoon. She was overjoyed to see Rose, but she knew there must be something behind the visit or Rose wouldn't have come down, for even though the violence was lessening, it was still a risk, Clara thought, coming all the way from Highdam.

'Rose, something happen? You dream something. Why you come down so sudden?' she asked a little fearfully.

'Look, a woman come all the way from Highdam and you asking stupid questions. Bring me something to drink, yeh girl, the heat killing.' Rose chuckled to put Clara at ease.

Clara began to fuss all over her, making some lime drink, taking her around the house, insisting that she go and have a lie-down in the children's bedroom, put her feet up while she got her something to eat.

151

But they had too much to catch up on. Rose followed her into the kitchen and while Clara rustled up some floats to go with the saltfish and pumpkin stew which she had left back from the midday meal, the two women began to fill each other in on all the happenings since their last parting.

It was like old times. The kitchen sink was piled up with unwashed plates and bowls, but Clara knew she didn't have to apologise to Rose for anything. As she fried the floats, her eyes moving from stove to Rose's face, Clara talked about the Georgetown life. About the choke-and-robbers, about the Charlestown yard, 'Girl, this yard full of melody and drama. If it isn't a big quarrel and loud dukebox music next door, is talk about burning down the Indian rumshop in front. One night we had to stay up until four in the morning, and the children in the thick of everything . . .'

As Rose ate Clara watched her with a smiling fullness, still feeling a bit uneasy. She knew Rose too well. This woman who seemed to be in touch with life's hidden forces. Who felt if there was good, then there must be evil, and who took the necessary precautions to deal with it. This woman who didn't have much faith in doctors.

As soon as Rose was finished eating Clara began again. 'You must have dreamt something about me, Rose. I know you too well.'

'You's an excitable woman, you know,' said Rose, studying Clara. 'You look like you lose weight,' she continued critically, as though her eyes saw into the restless nights that Clara was accustomed to having these days.

'You ain't change a bit,' said Clara, smiling. 'Look girl, tell me what you have to tell me. I can take it. You dream carrion crow flying round mih house? You dream the roof fall in? You dream mih teeth fall out?'

'Nothing as bad as that,' said Rose, 'But you have to be careful. Ah dream you was walking on a road, you one and ah didn't like the way you was looking. You was wearing a white dress, and you look so pale.'

'A white dress,' said Clara, her heart fluttering, 'a bridal dress?'

'I din say a bridal dress,' said Rose, 'I just say a white dress. So you have to be careful, you know white and sickness.'

'Coming to think of it,' said Clara, 'I've been having these funny feeling in my head. A kind of heaviness.'

'Presshah,' said Rose, 'that's how it does begin, presshah in de blood.' Rose produced the two parcels of bush, slightly withered, that she had brought for Clara. 'Some Blue Vine and a little Buck-Zeb-Grass. Boil a few pieces of each. Take half a glass morning. Half before bed at night.'

As she rested the tea bush on the table, Clara felt a warm relaxing glow, almost as if Rose had presented her with an ally against some unforeseen enemy. Now Clara was all eager to catch up on Highdam.

'Teacher Claudie is headmistress now,' began Rose, 'but everybody saying de standard of education drop since Teach leave.'

'Archie's head will feel big to hear that,' said Clara.

'Julie marry to Cyril,' continued Rose. 'Ida, Mister Watson granddaughter, gone off her head, running up and down the public road every full moon night like a horse. Watson himself sick. Ah hear they saying is cancer. Lawrence, that bright boy who was teaching when you husband was there, he gone away to England.'

Clara was listening hungrily.

'What about Dee-Dee?' she asked, 'she still visit Highdam?'

'Not since the troubles,' said Rose.

The troubles. They couldn't avoid the troubles. 'Girl is what happening to this country nuh?' asked Clara. 'How we get like this? I mean, the two races always had their differences. But we've also been living together and helping one another. Some of my best friends were East Indians when I was living in Essequibo. Now all the senseless killing.'

'It's the wicked ones on both sides that doing the mischief,' said Rose, 'some of them using the chance to settle old scores, as they say. Well it look as though things quietening down. We only have to hope and pray.'

Rose went on to tell Clara of some of the stories that the newspapers hadn't picked up on. But even in times of trouble the two women had preserved a place for laughter.

When Clara told Rose about the two left-side shoes that old Mr Castello got off the looting, and how he wore them mashed down at the back, Rose had a good laugh, throwing her head into Clara's lap.

And shortly after they heard the clicking of the front gate which announced Archie's arrival, back from a trip to the library.

'Eh, eh, Teach,' Rose welcomed him effusively as he walked through the front door.

'Aye, Rose, it's been a long time,' said Archie, who was caught completely by surprise at her unexpected presence. Surprised too, that for the first time, he was genuinely glad to see her.

When was the last time anyone had called him 'Teach'? As Archie sat listening to Rose, glancing across at the little smile on Clara's face from time to time, for a moment he felt as if they hadn't moved from Highdam at all.

Sometimes on your way from school you and Anthony would stop a little to gaze at the burnt-out house where Teddy lived. People still stop to gaze at the house and to talk about it in hushed voices. But no one would ever go inside the gate. Sometimes you spend a longer time than other times. Looking at the house of ruins. Wondering if Teddy spirit could still be hiding somewhere in there.

And your twelfth birthday coming up. And new elections coming up. And the beatings and killings have stopped. But your mother say, 'Only time can heal the wounds.' You hardly buy fluties these days, they're too red and sugary. Lurleena tells you that rubbing your breasts with the inside of yellow plantain skin would make them get bigger. You have to warm up the skin first though. Both of you try it for a while but no improvement. Still, your mother would say, 'Aye, you fulling eye, you fulling eye,' in an amused kind of way, when she come into the room and catch you looking at yourself in the mirror.

Conrad still comes often but you hardly sit in his lap anymore. Not because your mother would say,

'You're too big for that now,' but because you feel like being for yourself. Preliminary Exams coming up too, the first exams before entering secondary school. And your house is up for sale. Quite a few people come to look at it. Your father look at it too, walking round it, looking at it from the back garden where everything is blooming. The gooseberry tree laden with fat gooseberries, the pumpkins swelling big and heavy on the ground, the tomatoes ripe and plenty, and the bora climbing fresh and green as if it didn't care that the person who had planted it would be leaving.